Dressed to Kill

PETER CHEYNEY

Dressed to Kill
Peter Cheyney
First published as Night Club
by Poynings Press, UK in 1945
This production Copyright © 2022
Cover by Mats Ingelborn
with photo Pugoviuca88, Shutterstock
ISBN paper: 978-91-89225-59-6
ISBN e-book: 978-91-89225-60-2
ISBN audiobook: 978-91-89225-61-9
Published by Yabot AB, Stockholm, 2022

I. -- The Gentleman With Nerves

AS Gaunt closed the front street door of his office, the rain came. Standing in the doorway, turning up his coat collar, he grinned as he saw the trim figure of his secretary, Josephine Dark, on her way to the bus, battling with the wind which wrapped her skirts about her slim legs with an uncouth hand.

He felt in his overcoat pocket for a cigarette, cupped his lighter with his hands and lit it. As he put the lighter back into his pocket he turned his wrist and looked at the illuminated dial of his wrist-watch. Zona had telephoned at ten o'clock. Josephine, on Gaunt's instructions, had handled the call herself, saying that Gaunt would call at The Silver Ring at eleven o'clock.

It was a quarter-past. Gaunt, stepping out into the wet street thought cynically that it would do Zona good to stew for another three-quarters of an hour. Clients who telephoned through at night, with obvious nerves, were always the better for a little waiting, less inclined to argue about the fee.

At the Bruton Street intersection, he waited in the shelter of an awning for a cab. He was thirty-eight, six feet in height; his face was long and thin and his eyes big, brown and peculiarly luminous. His clothes were expensive and sat well on the square shoulders that tapered down to a thin waist and hips. You noticed his jaw. It was long, protruding and squared off at the end under a cynical mouth set beneath a flexible nose. Men looked at Gaunt's face because of his jaw and women because of the mouth.

Waiting for the cab he began to think about Zona. He wondered why Zona should be jittery. If there was anybody in the West End of London clever enough not to have to be jittery it was Mario Zona. Gaunt thought that maybe the trouble was woman trouble. Even the toughest hombres got scared of women.

He grinned at the thought and one or two associations that it brought to his mind. Then he remembered Ricket.

Would Ricket have something to say about Zona? The last time that Gaunt had seen the Detective-Inspector, with whom he was on terms of friendly enmity, Ricket had mentioned Zona's name, had made a remark about The Silver Ring Club.

A cab came round the corner. Gaunt stepped in. He told the driver to take him to the Calves Club. In the cab he lit another cigarette and relaxed.

Five minutes afterwards he opened the green

　　　　　　　　　　　　　　　Peter Cheyney

painted door on the third floor of a building in a street off Berkeley Square. Inside a narrow hall, sitting behind a desk, was Soames--the proprietor. He grinned at the private detective.

"Good-evening," said Gaunt "I suppose Mr. Ricket wouldn't be here?"

Soames grinned wryly. "He's here all right." He shrugged his shoulders glumly. "What the hell's the use of trying to run a club in the West End these days," he grumbled. "Either the place is full of people with no cash, or coppers who scare the people who have got money."

"Too bad," said Gaunt.

He walked across the hall, down the narrow passage and pushed aside the curtain at the end. At the bar, talking to a florid-faced individual in a brown bowler hat, was Ricket. Gaunt ordered a drink at the bar, carried it to a deserted table at the end of the room. He sat down and waited.

He had not long to wait. Three minutes afterwards Ricket, having disposed of the individual in the brown bowler, came over, a glass of lager beer in his hand. He sat down opposite Gaunt.

"Well, Rufus?' he said. "And how's the detective business?"

Gaunt grinned. "You ought to know," he said. "You're a real one. And how is Detective-Inspector Ricket? Still worrying about those racecourse boys?"

Ricket smiled. He put out two chubby fingers and took a cigarette that Gaunt offered.

"They're all right," he said. "We've got that lot in the bag. What are you doing round here? Another blackmailing case?"

"I don't know," said Gaunt. His face took on an expression of complete innocence. "As a matter of fact," he went on, "'I'm on my way round to see Zona. He telephoned through tonight."

The police officer raised his eyebrows. "What's the matter with him?" he asked casually--too casually.

"Search me," said the private detective. "He sounded a little bit scared--at least that's what my secretary told me."

Ricket smiled again. "Things must be getting pretty tough if Zona's scared," he said.

He lit the, cigarette and looked at Gaunt through the flame of the match.

"You know, Rufus," he said, "I've got a sort of liking for you in spite of the fact that you've pulled one or two chestnuts out of the fire in your time--a process that hasn't done me too much good. But I'd hate to see you make a real mistake."

Gaunt looked at him blankly. "You don't say," he said. "And what do you mean by a real mistake, Ricket?"

"Well," said Ricket, "you remember that

Stanford job last year. We had a cut-and-dried case against Stanford; the Commissioner had given instructions that I was to go ahead and arrest him. Then at the last moment you produced that alibi. That alibi was a fake and you know it, but it kept Stanford out of prison."

Gaunt grinned. "I think you've got it wrong. Ricket," he said. "I wouldn't do a thing like that."

Ricket blew out a mouthful of smoke. "Like hell, you wouldn't," he said. "Anyhow, I want to tell you something, and I wouldn't like you to forget it, Rufus, because even a private investigator who's as clever as you are is wise to keep his nose clean with Scotland Yard. There are one or two people down there waiting to jump on you."

"Well... well…!" said Gaunt. "What do I do now? Take something to build my nerves up? And why do I have to be careful about Zona?"

Ricket finished his lager beer. "I'm not giving away any secrets," he said, "when I tell you that Zona's been sailing pretty close to the wind for the last six months. Who does he think he is to get away with the stuff that he's been pulling at that Silver Ring Club? And did you know about the place at Manchester?"

"No," said Gaunt casually. "Tell me about it."

"He's got a gaming house just outside Manchester--it's one of a string," the detective-inspector went on. "There's one in Birmingham, one in Bristol, three in Glasgow, and probably a dozen more that we don't know about. All sorts of funny business has been going on at these places, and we've even had some complaints! People have been stung so hard that they were prepared to risk bad publicity in order to get their own back on Zona. I'm not interested in the provinces but I am interested in The Silver Ring. It's a bad club. I'd like to close it."

Gaunt yawned. "Some very nice people go round there," he said. "The food is good and they tell me the cabaret is wonderful. Have you ever seen the cabaret, Ricket?" asked Gaunt blandly.

"No, I haven't," said Ricket, "and I don't particularly want to. I'm not interested in what goes on at that club up to one o'clock in the morning. My interest starts after that time--from about one-thirty to four."

Gaunt took out his cigarette-case, lit another cigarette slowly. "Now I wonder why you're telling me all this, Ricket," he said. He smiled across the table. "You know that I'm probably going to be working for Zona. He hasn't rung me up for me to go round there and discuss the weather with him, you know."

Ricket shrugged. "I don't care if you tell Zona," he said.

Gaunt raised his eyebrows. "You mean you've

got a case against him?" he asked.

The policeman grinned. "Not particularly," he said, "but it looked to me as if our friend Mario Zona has created an organisation which he used to run and which is now running him. In other words, he's started something which he can't stop. Possibly that's why he sounded scared on the telephone."

Gaunt pursed his lips. "You mean he's so far in that he can't get out?" he said.

Ricket nodded. "Something like that." He got up. "Well, good-night, Rufus, I'll be seeing you some time, and don't forget, watch your step."

IT was twelve o'clock when Gaunt paid off his cab at the Regent Street end of Brookes Passage. The rain had stopped, but the wind was still howling dismally. He walked along the passage and knocked on the door which faced him at the far end.

After a minute or two the grille in the door opened and a face looked out. Then the grille shut and the door opened. Gaunt walked down the long passage that traversed the width of the building. At the end he took a lift to the third floor. As he got out of the lift there came to him through the heavy velvet curtains opposite a sound of subdued swing music played by a good band.

He pushed aside the curtain, handed his overcoat

and hat to the girl dressed as a page-boy who looked after the cloakroom, pushed open the swing doors and walked on to the main floor of The Silver Ring.

Gaunt was standing on a balcony three or four feet from the floor. The balcony ran round three sides of the room. There was a pass door at each end which bounded the heavy curtains drawn across the band platform at the far end of the dance floor.

The place was in semi-darkness, but from the tables set on the balcony came an occasional tinkling of a glass or a whispered remark. A single spot-lime worked from above made a brilliant circle of light in the middle of the floor, and Gaunt's mouth curved into a smile as he looked at the girl who stood in it. He wondered how it was that Zona always got good-lookers like that, and as he listened to her song, the detective realised that Zona had got something more than a good-looker this time.

She was of good height, supple, curved in all the right places. Her face was more than beautiful; her hair, titian red, served as a superb frame for the whiteness of her face.

Gaunt fumbled in his pocket for a loose cigarette and listened, appreciating the subdued tempo of the orchestra.

As the girl stopped singing the lights went up. Gaunt signalled the head waiter.

"I'm Rufus Gaunt," he said, "I think Mr. Zona's

waiting to see me."

He followed the man round the right-hand wing of the balcony, through the glass door.

The head waiter indicated the white door ahead of him. Gaunt opened it, stepped into Zona's office, grinned at Zona, who sat behind a big walnut desk set diagonally across the corner of the grey and black office.

Mario Zona was fat, fifty, looked--and was--very tough. Two steel-blue eyes twinkled brightly from a face, the top half of which was near Asiatic. His hands, white, plump, well-cared for, lay loosely on the desk in front of him, emerging from snowy cuffs linked by diamond cuff-links the size of farthings.

Gaunt walked over to the desk. He flipped open a cigarette box, took out a cigarette and lit it. He sat on the corner of the desk.

"Good evening, Zona," he said.

Zona looked up. He was smiling, but he seemed to produce the smile with an effort. He put his hand down and opened a drawer in the desk, brought out a bottle of liqueur brandy and two small glasses. He filled them. Gaunt brought a chair from the other side of the room, set it down directly in front of the desk and sat down.

Zona pushed a glass towards him and began to speak. He spoke slowly and quietly in careful English.

"You listen to me, Mr. Gaunt," he said, "because what I am going to say to you is rather important. You understand?"

Gaunt nodded. "That's what they all say," he said. "Get on with it, and cut out the frills. Then I'll tell you whether or not I'll do it."

He blew a smoke ring, watched it sail across the room.

"All right," said Zona evenly. "I'm frightened, that's all."

"That's definite enough," said Gaunt. "What are you frightened of?"

Zona said: "Did you see the girl who was singing when you came in? That's Meralda Grey. I knew that girl's father. He did me a good turn once. So I gave her a chance here, and she's made good. She's a nice girl. I'm fond of her, you understand that?"

"I understand," said Gaunt.

"Six months ago, when she was singing at my place in Manchester," Zona went on, "she fell in love with someone--at least she thought she fell in love with him. He looked a very nice man, a sensible fellow. So because I was fond of her I gave him a job. His name s Lorimer--Michael Lorimer. He's my manager."

Zona picked up the glass of liqueur brandy and sipped it delicately.

"I brought him up here because he'd worked

very well in Manchester," he continued. "I gave him a job of looking after all my places." He spread his hands. "I don't have to tell you that sometimes there is a little gambling goes on in places like this, Mr. Gaunt. Little parties that go on after the cabaret is over and the club is closed. That's how we make our money. His business was to check and supervise the takings of the different clubs.

"Three months ago, I noticed some discrepancies in the accounts. I spoke to him about it, but nothing happened. The discrepancies went on. Somebody has been systematically robbing me. I have good reason to believe that it's Lorimer,"

"Well, you don't need a detective to tell you what to do for that," he said. "All you have to do is to kick him out."

Zona spread his hands again. 'That's not so easy," he said, "he might know too much."

Gaunt raised his eyebrows. "Might?" he queried.

Zona drank a little more brandy

"Two weeks ago," he said, "I thought it my duty to warn Meralda that I thought she was making a bad mistake about Lorimer; that he was no good. She didn't take my advice kindly. She was very angry with me. I have good reason to believe that she told him what I had said. Since then one or two strange things have happened. Somebody turned the gas fire on--without bothering to light it--in my apartment whilst I was asleep one night. Luckily for me my bedside telephone rang in the small hours of the morning, otherwise I'd probably be dead now. I think that was Lorimer."

"I see," said Gaunt. "So you think he wants you out of the way. Why?"

"I'll tell you," said Zona. "Three or four weeks ago I thought it might be to my advantage to make me inquiries into the past of our Mr. Lorimer. I received certain information which does not matter at the moment. I think it is possible he knows I have it. I don't think Lorimer would like anybody, especially the police, to have that information. I think he will stop at nothing to get me out of the way."

Gaunt blew another smoke ring. "All right," he said. "What am I supposed to do?"

Zona bent down and opened a drawer. He took out a packet of banknotes. He pushed them across the desk towards the detective.

"There are five hundred pounds there," he said. "I want you to look after me. Tomorrow evening I shall have some free time. I should like to talk to you. I should like to tell you everything about this business. Perhaps you could come and see me."

Gaunt got up. "All right," he said. "When and where?"

"Perhaps you could come at half-past seven," said

Zona getting up. He looked a little easier. "I live at the Colindale Apartments off Berkeley Square."

"I know," said Gaunt. "I'll be there at seven-thirty. Goodnight."

He put the packet of banknotes into his breast pocket, walked to the door and opened it. As he stepped through, he found himself face to face with the girl who had been singing. He grinned amiably.

"Good-evening, Miss Grey," he said. "I liked that song of yours."

She looked at him. He could see that her mouth was set in a straight line with temper. Her blue eyes were blazing.

"I suppose you're Mr. Gaunt," she said, "The famous Mr. Rufus Gaunt--possibly Zona's new bodyguard?"

Gaunt closed the door gently behind him. "And you don't think Mr Zona needs a bodyguard, Miss Grey?" he queried.

"I do not," she flung back at him, "and I do not appreciate this pretty little plot that he's building up against Michael. I'm not going to stand for it."

Gaunt grinned. "No?" he said. "And what are you going to do about it?"

"I'll find something to do, Mr. Gaunt," she said. "Zona had better take care. He's going too far."

Gaunt's voice was very soft. "You don't like Mr. Zona," he said, "do you?"

She looked him in the eye. "Not particularly," she said. "Perhaps I'm only just beginning to find out one or two things about him--about the man who's always professed to be my father's friend and my own."

Gaunt said easily: "That's very interesting. Why--if you're so keen on Lorimer--don't you come and tell me about it? I'll be in my office in Conduit Street at five o'clock tomorrow. Or would you consider that walking into the lion's den?"

She tossed her head. "I'm not afraid of you or anyone else, Mr. Gaunt," she said. "And I'd like you to know that if Zona or anyone else tried to frame Michael I'd stop at nothing!"

Gaunt grinned. "And I suppose you were on your way to tell Zona that," he said. "Well... don't let me stop you. "Good night, Miss Grey."

II. -- The Girl With a Gun

WHEN Josephine Dark came into the office Gaunt was in his usual position, slumped down in the armchair by the fire with his feet on the mantelpiece, busily engaged in blowing smoke rings.

"Miss Meralda Grey is outside said Josephine primly. "And by the look of her I don't think you're too popular!"

Gaunt grinned. "If I was a popular sort of person I'd wonder why," he said. "Show her in."

He took his feet off the mantelpiece and seated himself at his desk, the cigarette hanging out of the corner of his mouth.

Meralda Grey came in. Gaunt shot a quick glance at her, took in the superbly cut suit, the expensive gloves, the small, beautifully shaped feet, the luxurious silver fox fur that framed the white oval of her face. He got up and pushed the cigarette box towards her.

"Sit down, Miss Grey," he said.

"Have a cigarette, and I'll ring for a cup of tea for you." He pressed his desk bell.

"Thank you," she said, "but..."

"Never mind," said Gaunt, still grinning. "Don't you think that we might as well make up our minds to be friends?"

She threw back her furs. The detective, still looking at her, was trying to remember just when he had seen a woman as attractive as this one.

"Is it possible for us to be friends, Mr. Gaunt?" she asked.

Josephine Dark brought in the tea. Gaunt waited until she had gone, then he stood his with back to the fireplace smiling at Meralda Grey.

"I don't see any reason why we shouldn't be quite good friends," he said amiably. "You see, Miss Grey, there are two kinds of private detectives--one that believes that the client must always be right, and the other kind who prefers to keep an open mind. I've got an open mind. Supposing that you and I both put our cards down on the table, don't you think it might help?"

She thought for a moment, then:

"Why not? And perhaps I ought to apologise. I was rude to you last night."

"Don't worry about that," said Gaunt. "You were feeling angry. You've got quite a temper, haven't you, sometimes...?"

She smiled. Gaunt noticed the beauty of her little white teeth.

"I am afraid I have," she said. "That's my failing, but it never lasts very long."

"All right," said Gaunt. "Well, now we know where we are. You've got a temper... sometimes, and

I've got an open mind. Now I'm going to put my cards down with you. Maybe I've only heard one side of this story--Zona's side. Zona says he gave Michael Lorimer--to whom I understand you are engaged--a job in Manchester some months ago for your sake. He says that somebody has been doing him down badly and he suspects Lorimer.

"He says that he's taken the trouble to check on Lorimer's record and apparently he's found it is a pretty bad one. He says that Lorimer knows this and as a result of knowing it he's dangerous. It seems that somebody turned the gas fire in Zona's bedroom.on one night without lighting it. He thinks that was Lorimer, too. He says he doesn't want to get rid of Lorimer because he might know too much. That's his side of the story. And you don't believe any part of it?"

Her mouth set in a decided line.

"It's nothing but a tissue of lies--beastly lies, Mr. Gaunt," she said. "Michael is the finest man in the world. I ought to know. I'm going to marry him. Now let me give you my side of the story.

"I began to work for Mr. Zona quite a time ago. I was glad to get the opportunity. I always wanted to be a singer, and here was my chance. Mr. Zona had always professed to be a friend of my father's. I believed that because at the time there was no reason why I shouldn't. Now I don't believe it.

"I met Michael when I was singing at Zona's club--the Pirates Club--in Manchester. Zona saw me with him, asked about him. I told him that Michael and I were in love with each other.

"Mr. Zona seemed very kind. He suggested that Michael should come and work for him. He said it would be nice for us both."

"You think he had some ulterior motive in that?" Gaunt queried.

"I'm certain of it now," she answered. "I'm firmly convinced that Zona employed Michael because Michael had had no previous experience of night clubs. He knew nothing about them. Zona looked on him as a young fool who could go into the Manchester club as manager and who, if anything went wrong, would bear the brunt of it, would take the responsibility which should rightly fall on Zona's own shoulders."

"Bear the brunt of what, Miss Grey?" asked Gaunt. He threw his cigarette end in the fire and lit another.

"I'm not quite certain," she said. "But Michael knows, and he won't say."

Gaunt smoked silently for a few minutes. He was thinking of his conversation with Detective-Inspector Ricket on the night before. He was wondering whether Lorimer had by chance found out what Ricket suspected.

"Have you any ideas about what was going on?" he said.

She shook her head. "I don't know. I can only guess that something illegal was happening at night after the club was officially closed--gambling or something of that sort. I can only guess that Michael found out--that he was torn between a feeling of loyalty to me, and possibly to Zona, and his duty. I believe that Michael has told Zona that he knows and has suggested that this illegal business, whatever it may be, has got to stop. I think that frightened Zona, and I think it isn't only Zona who has to be considered. There are other people--his odd friends and associates--who may think that Michael knows too much."

"I see," said Gaunt. "And so you believe that this telephone call to me from Zona last night was the first move in a plot to frame Michael?"

She nodded. "I'm certain of it," she said.

Gaunt walked over to the window and looked out. It was dark outside and in the circles of light made by the street lamps he could see the rain teeming down.

He said: "Tell me something. Why didn't Lorimer come up here with you today? Don't you think that if what you say is right, that there ought to be a show-down about this business? It seems to me that everybody is running round in circles.

You're afraid of something, your boy friend is afraid of something and Zona is afraid of something. So am I!"

She smiled unhappily. "You don't seem to be the sort of man who'd be easily frightened. Mr. Gaunt," she said. "What are you afraid of?"

Gaunt grinned. "Merely that I won't get at the truth," he said. "Or that I'll get it so late that something odd will happen before I have time to do anything about it. But you haven't answered my question. Why didn't Lorimer come up here with you this afternoon?"

"There is an excellent reason," she said. "He's not in London. I sent him away."

Gaunt raised his eyebrows.

"Perhaps that looks suspicious to you, Mr. Gaunt," she said. "I thought then I saw a glint of distrust come into your eyes. I had great difficulty in persuading Michael to leave London, but I thought it was the best thing for everybody concerned. I believed that at this moment the best thing Michael could do would be to leave Zona, to go back to Manchester, to try to get his old job back again--to get out of this atmosphere of suspicion and distrust. Don't you think it was wise?"

"No, I don't," said Gaunt. "If he was in danger when he was with Zona, he'll be in greater danger if he's not there. While he was there at least Zona and

                    Peter Cheyney

Company--that is supposing your theory is correct--could keep their eye on him."

She nodded. "So you're coming round to my point of view, Mr. Gaunt?" she said.

Gaunt shook his head. "Oh, no, Miss Grey," he said. "I'm working for Zona; I've taken his money. Up to the moment I've no reason to believe that anything he's told me hasn't been the truth. Mind you"--he grinned cynically--"a lot of people seem to think that he's a crook. Maybe I'll be thinking the same thing myself. We'll see."

He took another cigarette from the silver box on his desk. "And Michael didn't mind leaving you--he didn't think that you were in any danger?" he said.

"Oh, yes, he did," she answered. "I had a great deal of trouble to persuade him to go. He said that he believed that Zona and his friends would stop at nothing; that if they thought that I knew anything, they'd be quite relentless with me. That's why Michael told me to carry a pistol. She tapped her handbag.

Gaunt pursed his lips. "As bad as that, eh? Do you know anything about pistols, Miss Grey?" he asked.

She smiled. "Quite a bit," she said. "I'm a good pistol shot, although I've never used a gun like this one."

"Let me look at it," said Gaunt. She opened her

handbag, produced a flat blued steel automatic 0.32 Colt. Gaunt walked over to her, took the weapon from her hand, looked at it.

"These are nice guns," he said. "I've got one like this myself. This one has the newest form of safety catch on it, but I doubt if it is as good as the old type. Just a minute."

He opened a door, went into an inner office, and returned after a minute or two with another automatic. He explained the difference in the two guns to her. He pointed out the mechanism of the new type of safety catch. Then he handed the gun back to her.

"Lorimer may be right," he said. "It might be a good thing for you to have a gun. But I don't think so." He grinned. "I've always found that it is the people who carry guns who get shot," he said.

He went back and stood in front of the fireplace. "Well, what's the next move in a game?" he asked.

A determined look came into her eyes. "I've made up my mind, Mr. Gaunt," she said. "There's got to be a show-down. I thought it all out this morning before I got Michael to go away. I'm going to have a show-down with Zona. I'm going to get the truth from him one way or another. I'm going to stop this ridiculous business. I'm going to ensure Michael's safety and my own,"

Gaunt said: "Aren't you being a little bit dramatic,

Miss Grey? Do you think this business is really as serious as you make out?"

She nodded. "I do," she said. "I've been on the telephone to Zona this afternoon. I'm going round to see him at his flat at seven o'clock. Things are going to be settled one way or another. I'm going to tell him that whatever happens, nothing that I can do to protect Michael shall be left undone,"

Gaunt said nothing. He was thinking of his own appointment with Zona at seven-thirty. There was a pause. They could hear the rain pattering on the windows. Then Gaunt said:

"Let me give you a tip Miss Grey. Don't go and see Zona. Leave this business alone."

"Why do you say that?" she asked.

He shrugged his shoulders. "Call it a hunch if you like," he said. "But I told you I'd put my cards on the table with you and I will. I've got an appointment with Zona myself tonight at seven-thirty. We're going to have a long talk together. Maybe I can clear all this business up. Maybe something of what you say is true. Zona's a tough specimen. Possibly he's been sailing a little too close to the wind, but nothing that matters a great deal. Perhaps when I've heard what he's got to say I could give you some good advice. I think that would be the best way of dealing with it, don't you?"

She got up. "No, I don't, Mr. Gaunt," she said.

"Possibly you have been honest with me. In any event I'm going to be honest with you. I've nothing to hide. I don't know whose side you're on at this moment, but I do know that you're working for Zona, and until I know I can trust you I'm not going to take any risks. I won't take a chance on my own and Michael's happiness. I shall see Zona tonight. I intend to settle this business one and for all."

Gaunt grinned. "All right, Miss Grey," he said. "You have your own way. Tell me something--what time do you go to The Silver Ring Club at night?"

"Not till fairly late," she answered, arranging her furs. "I get there usually about eleven-thirty."

"I see," said Gaunt. "Well, I've a suggestion to make. Have dinner with me at nine o'clock tonight. We'll both have seen Zona. Maybe we can exchange a few more ideas to our mutual good. What about it?"

She looked at him. He was glad to see she was smiling.

"There are moments when I quite like you, Mr. Gaunt," she said. "Yes, I'd like to have dinner with you. Thank you."

"Excellent," said Gaunt. "We'll meet at the Laurel Restaurant at nine o'clock. I'll be waiting for you. Is that all right?"

"That will be very nice," she said. "Good evening.

Mr. Gaunt."

He held the door for her as she went out of the office. Then he went back to his armchair and began blowing more smoke rings.

AT six o'clock the telephone in the outer office jangled. The buzzer on Gaunt's desk flickered. He took off the receiver.

"Mr. Zona's on the line," said Josephine Dark. "He wants to talk to you. He says its urgent."

"All right," said Gaunt. "Put him through."

He waited. Zona came on the line. His voice was hoarse and rasping.

"What's the matter with you, Zona?" asked Gaunt. "You don't sound very good to me."

"I don't feel very good, Mr. Gaunt," said Zona. "I've got a bad cold. I'm staying in my flat today."

Gaunt grinned. "Look after it," he said. "It would be a pity if you got pneumonia. You might die."

Zona said: "I might die of other things besides pneumonia, Mr. Gaunt. I rang you up because I wanted to tell you I had a telephone call this afternoon. Somebody's been working on Meralda Grey."

Gaunt said: "I don't understand."

"You will, Mr. Gaunt," Zona went on. "Someone's been talking poison to her. That girl's got a bad temper. She can be dangerous. At four o'clock this afternoon she rang me up. She used very threatening language. She told me that she'd got Lorimer out of London; that I couldn't get at him; that for the time being anyway he was safe. She warned me not to try and find out where he was. She said, that if I tried to make things tough for Michael she'd kill me!"

III. -- Exit Zona!

IT was a quarter to seven. Gaunt stood at the window looking out into Conduit Street. The rain had stopped, but the wet street still reflected the glow of the street lamps. He yawned, walked back to his desk, lit a cigarette and rang for Josephine Dark.

When she came in he said: "We've got a nice case, Josephine."

She smiled. "Meaning just what?" she asked.

"Meaning that I'm wondering what I am being employed for," said Gaunt. "I've been paid--very well paid--to look after Zona, who's afraid of Lorimer, who's afraid of Zona, it's just one of those things."

He grinned at her. She smiled back.

"It sounds like a case for you," she said.

Gaunt walked over to the fireplace. "You get on the telephone to Rendle in Manchester," he ordered. "Tell him to try and get a line on Zona's club up there--the Pirates Club. Tell Rendle to play it very quietly, not to worry about what goes on in the club up till the official closing time, but to try to find out what happens after that time. Tell him I'd like to hear from him as soon as possible."

"And after that?" she queried.

"After that you can go home," said Gaunt with a grin.

She closed her notebook and left the office. Gaunt went back to his armchair by the fireside, put his feet in their usual position on the mantelpiece. He was wondering about two or three odd points in his conversation with Zona of the night before and his talk with Meralda Grey that afternoon. He was think about an odd incongruity or two--little points that did not quite match in the story.

Five minutes passed. Outside in the outer office he could hear Josephine Dark talking to Rendle in Manchester. He ruminated on the fact that she possessed a charming voice.

Just then the telephone rang. Gaunt took off the receiver on his desk and answered it. It was Meralda Grey!

"Is that Mr. Gaunt?" she said.

Gaunt said it was. He was surprised. There was something in the quality of her voice that was almost startling--a hard, frightened note.

"What's the matter?" he said. "Is anything wrong?"

She began to laugh, a fearful sort of laugh, a high hysterical laugh. She stopped quite suddenly, then she said in a very cold, controlled voice:

"There's quite a lot wrong, Mr. Gaunt. I've killed Zona."

Gaunt moved his cigarette to the other side of his mouth. "You're not dreaming or anything, are you?" he said. "Or you're not even trying to be funny? Do you mean that?"

"Yes, I do," she said. "I've shot him. He's dead. It's terrible, isn't it? What am I going to do?"

Gaunt thought for a moment.

Then he said quite coolly: "It's rather a pity that you didn't think of that before you shot Zona. Where are you?"

She gulped. "I'm in the cocktail bar at the Laurel," she said. "I came here directly."

Gaunt said: "All right. Now listen, just don't do anything at all. Sit down and have a drink. I suggest lime-juice because you sound rather hysterical. I'm coming right round. I'll be with you in five minutes."

"Very well," she said. "I'll wait for you. Please be quick."

Gaunt hung up the receiver. He threw his cigarette into the fire and stood for a moment looking into the dying embers. Then he walked over to the hat-stand in the corner of his office and put on his hat and coat. As he went through the outer office Josephine had just finished her call to Manchester.

She said: "Sorry you had to take that call. I was talking to Rendle."

Gaunt grinned. "That's all right," he said. "I like getting calls direct sometimes. There's always the chance that an odd call might be amusing. Good night, Jose."

"Goodnight, Mr. Gaunt," she said softly.

He closed the door behind him.

MERALDA Grey was sitting at the table furthest from the bar in the cocktail room at the Laurel. On the table was an untouched drink. She was looking straight in front of her, smoking a cigarette. She sat quite still, staring as if she saw a ghost.

Gaunt walked to the bar and ordered a whisky and soda to be brought over to him. He walked across and sat beside her.

"Well?" he said. This doesn't sound so good to me. First of all, is it true?"

She nodded dumbly. Then she ran her tongue over her lips. Gaunt sensed that her mouth was dry with fear.

"Well," he said, "You'd better tell me how it happened. It must have been rather sudden."

She nodded again.

"Have your drink," said Gaunt. "I should think you need it. And take it easy. Don't let's start worrying… yet."

She picked up the glass. He could see that her fingers were trembling. She gulped a little of the drink and put the glass back on the table.

"Now," said Gaunt, and his voice . was soft and

low and persuasive, "let's hear all about it.",

He took out his cigarette case. "Smoke a cigarette," he said. "It might help." He lit the cigarette for her.

After a little while she said: "When I left your office this afternoon I took a cab. I went home. When I got there I found a typewritten note waiting for me. It was from Zona. Somehow, I don't know how, he knew that I'd been to see you. I suppose he'd been having me watched. It was a fearful note. It accused me of everything--disloyalty, underhand dealing, everything he could think of.

It went on to say that it was quite useless for me to endeavour to get behind his back; that he'd discovered that I'd sent Michael out of the way; that that wasn't going to help. He said that he'd found out all he wanted to find out about Michael; that he had enough on him to send him to prison for a considerable time; that he was going to do it and chance what happened as a result. He said that he thought that I was as bad as Michael was and that from now on he regarded me as an enemy. He said my appointment with him was cancelled--he didn't want to see me; that the best thing I could do would be to keep out of his way."

Gaunt nodded. "Have you got that note?" he said.

She shook her head. "I crumpled it up and threw

it in the fire. I didn't know what I was doing. But I knew that I had to see Zona. I was fearfully angry--I felt quite livid with rage. I dashed downstairs and took the first cab I saw. I went straight round to Zona's flat at the Colindale Apartments. He opened the door. He was grinning like a fiend.

"When I went inside I'd made up my mind I'd keep cool; that I wouldn't lose my temper. We went into his study--a room on the other side of the hall. He sat down at the desk. He didn't ask me to sit down. Then he asked what I wanted. I told him about the note. I said it was a fearful note to send to me. I asked him what he meant by it. Then he began to talk.

"He said the most terrible things. He made the most fearful accusations against Michael. He went further--he suggested that I'd been plotting with Michael; that we were both as bad as each other; that we'd done nothing ever since we'd been together working for Zona except to try and get behind his back. He suggested that Michael was responsible for all the illegal things that had been going on at the club; that he thought Zona couldn't do anything about it because he'd be afraid of blackmail.

"He said that was the reason he'd been forced to employ you. That, having done that, he'd discovered that I'd run true to form and had tried to get at you behind his back. He was quite awful.

"Then he said that I had good reason to be concerned for Michael; that before he was through with Michael he'd be in prison; that I could think myself lucky if I wasn't with him.

"I was trying to control myself. I gripped my handbag and I felt that pistol inside. I didn't know what I was doing. I took it out. I told Zona he was a liar, a crook; that he'd been using Michael merely as a front; that now that people--possibly the police--were beginning to find out something about him, he was going to use Michael as a scapegoat. I said he'd plotted that from the start; that he'd even used me in the same scheme; that it was through me he'd got Michael to work for him at all.

"I told him that if he didn't leave Michael and me alone I'd kill him. I showed him the pistol. He laughed. He said that I was a very good actress, but that my amateur dramatics meant nothing to him. He said some more things--terrible things.

"I don't think I've ever hated anybody so much in my life. I didn't know it was possible to hate anybody like I hated him. I aimed the pistol at him and fired.

"I was standing by the side of his desk--a few feet from him. He slumped forward. I saw the red mark on the left-hand side of his head.

"Suddenly I realised what I had done. I ran out of the room, closed the door behind me, crossed the hall, shut the front door and began to walk down the corridor. Every minute I thought I was going to faint. I didn't know what to do then I thought of you. I thought I'd telephone you.

"I went into a call box. Then I remembered the girl at the exchange might hear. I came outside, took a cab, came here and telephoned you from here."

She put her face between her hands and began to sob. Gaunt saw her shoulders heaving.

He smoked silently for a minute, watching her. Then he said with a wry smile: "It must be nice for Michael to have a woman so keen on him that she's prepared to kill for him. But it wasn't a very clever thing to do, was it? You'd better pull yourself together. Tears aren't going to do you any good now."

She said: "No, it wasn't very clever--it was just stupid. There is no hope now."

Gaunt grinned. "I wouldn't say that," he said. "While there's life there's hope. Where's the gun?"

She pulled herself together. "It's in my handbag," she said.

"Give it to me," said Gaunt. "Very quietly, so that no one sees."

She fumbled with the catch of her handbag, opened it, slipped the gun across the table to Gaunt. He put it in his pocket.

"What shall I do?" she said.

Gaunt blew a smoke ring and watched it.

"Nothing," he said. "Go home, lie down and try to relax. I'll get in touch with you."

She looked at him; her eyes were wide with fear.

"What are you going to do?" she asked.

Gaunt shrugged his shoulders. "I don't know," he said. "That depends on circumstances. But at the moment I'm going round to make certain that what you say is true. I'd like to have a look at Zona. You go home."

"Very well," she said. "But oughtn't I to give myself up? Shouldn't I go to the police?"

He grinned again. In some strange way she found comfort in that grin, and in the sight of the strong white teeth that showed when he smiled.

"There's lots of time for that," he said. "You go home. I'll get in touch with you. You'd better powder your nose. You look like nothing on earth."

Five minutes afterwards they left the Laurel. Outside, he put her in a cab; ordered the driver to take her to her flat. He walked into Regent Street, stopped another cab and told the man to go to Berkeley Square.

Gaunt stopped the taxi at the bottom of Hay Hill. He paid the man off, walked across the Square towards the Colindale Apartments. At the doorway he stopped, glad of the darkness which enabled him to see without being seen. He waited there for two or three minutes until, in response to the lift bell from one of the floors above, the hall porter took the lift up.

Gaunt pushed open the glass entrance door and walked into the hall. The indicator showed him that Zona's apartment was on the first floor. Gaunt walked quickly and quietly up the stairs, along the corridor. Again he was lucky--the entrance to Zona's rooms was round a left-angle bend in the corridor. The hall door formed a cul-de-sac.

Gaunt fumbled in his waistcoat pocket, from which he produced two small pieces of mica. He tore the mica into the rough shape of a key, inserted it in the lock, twisted and turned it until he felt the wards, of the lock grip against the mica; then he pulled it out and examined it. Marked on the transparent material were the indentations of the lock. He took a pair of scissors out of his pocket and began to cut the piece of mica. In less than two minutes he had the door open.

He stepped into the hall, closing the door behind him. The light was burning in the hall and Gaunt could see opposite him a closed door. He opened it and stepped into the room.

Zona was lying on the far side of his desk. The chair in which he had been sitting--a chair fitted with castors--had obviously slipped back as his body had fallen sideways. His knees were drawn up, his fingers clenched. There was a pool of blood beneath his head staining the fawn carpet.

Gaunt felt in his pocket for a cigarette and lit it. Then he drew on his gloves and began to walk about the room observing the layout of the furniture. He concentrated on the desk and the things that were on it.

At the far end of the wall behind the desk was a door. Gaunt opened it, switched on the light. The room was a bedroom. He examined the room cursorily, noticing that the double windows led out on to a fire escape running down to the street. He grinned. It was characteristic of Zona to have an apartment with a back way out.

He switched off the light, walked back into the study closing the bedroom door behind him. He stood for a few minutes smoking silently, thinking.

Then he put his hand in his pocket and brought out the Colt automatic pistol that Meralda Grey had given to him. He pulled out the ammunition clip, examined it, pulled back the ejector breech action of the gun, and smelt the barrel. One cartridge shell was missing. He found it by the desk, picked it up.

Then he examined the other nine shells in the clip. He grinned and put the gun back into his pocket.

He stood looking down at Zona, who would never run any more night clubs, thinking cynically that it was just as well that the Greek had paid him the five hundred pounds on account of professional services the night before.

On the other side of the study, the fire was still burning in the grate.

Gaunt threw his cigarette stub into the embers and lit another. Then he sat down in the leather armchair by the side of the fire and smoked.

Two or three minutes afterwards he got up. He stepped over to the telephone on the desk, dialled Whitehall 1212.

When Scotland Yard replied, he asked to speak to Detective-Inspector Ricket.

He was smiling--almost happily.

IV. -- Surprise No. 1

IT was eight o'clock when Gaunt heard the squad car stop outside the Colindale Apartments. He went into the hallway and opened the door. Then he went back to the study and stood, cigarette hanging out of the corner of his mouth, looking at Zona. He was there when Ricket came in.

Gaunt pointed to the body on the far side of the desk, and Ricket, with the unconcerned air of one to whom death and murder are merely part of the day's business, walked over and stood looking at what had once been Mario Zona.

"It was nice of you to ring through so quickly, Gaunt," he said eventually. "How did you happen to be here?"

Gaunt said: "I suppose you've got a surgeon and the photographers coming around?"

"In about twenty minutes' time," Ricket answered.

"All right," said Gaunt. He smiled amiably. "You know, Ricket, I always like putting my cards down."

Ricket also smiled. "You wouldn't forget that I've had previous experience of your process of putting your cards down? I wouldn't keep anything up your sleeve this time if I were you."

Gaunt said : "I don't intend to."

He offered his cigarette case to the Detective-Inspector.

"Smoke a cigarette and listen," he said. "I'll tell you what I know. Last evening as you know, Zona telephoned through to my office. He seemed frightened. He wanted to see me. I thought there might be a chance of seeing you at the Calves Club. I thought you might have something on Zona. So I dropped in on the off-chance. Well, you were there, and apparently you had got something on Zona. Incidentally, I don't think you were the only one."

Ricket raised his eyebrows. He had taken off his bowler hat and put it on the floor by the side of his chair.

"Meaning what?" he asked abruptly.

Gaunt went on: "I got to the Silver Ring Club about midnight last night," he said. "The first thing I noticed was the girl who was singing in the cabaret show--Meralda Grey. That girl's a honey if ever there was one. She's got everything.

"All right. I saw Zona. Zona was frightened; at least that's what he said, and I must say he looked the part. In effect he told me that he'd noticed certain shortages in the takings in The Silver Ring and in some of his provincial clubs. He suspected his manager--Michael Lorimer.

"Apparently Zona had given Lorimer the job because Meralda Grey, the cabaret star--the daughter of an old friend of Zona's--was keen on him.

"I told Zona that, if he suspected Lorimer, the thing to do was to kick him out. Zona suggested that wasn't possible; that Lorimer might know too much about something or other.

"That made me remember you, Ricket. I thought for a moment that Lorimer might have suspected some of the things about the Zona organisation that were interesting you. But Zona put a different complexion on that idea. He suggested that any illegalities in the clubs, either in London or in the provinces, had been started by Lorimer. He went further--he said that as a result of his suspicions about Lorimer he'd had his record checked. He discovered several things about the young man, things which Lorimer might not like to come to light. He suggested that Lorimer would do anything in order to stop him--Zona--talking."

Ricket nodded. "Very interesting," he said. "Go on, Rufus."

"I made an appointment to see Zona tonight at seven-thirty," Gaunt continued. "He was going to give me the whole story. When I was leaving his office I ran into the girl--Meralda Grey. Either she'd somehow heard of the telephone call which Zona had put through to my office or she'd been listening outside the door. In any event she knew what we'd been talking about. As I left she was going into his room. She intended to tell him what she thought about him.

"Just before she went in I suggested she might like to come and have a word with me in my office. I put the idea into her head that I was a rather open-minded fellow and liked to hear both sides of the story.

"Well, she came round this afternoon. She told me a very different story. In her story Zona was the villain and her fiancé Michael Lorimer was the hero. She had arranged to see Zona tonight at seven o'clock. She was angry with him and she was taking the matter pretty seriously. She'd got Lorimer to clear out of London because she said she knew Zona was trying to frame him.

"I thought that between the conversation she was to have with Zona at seven o'clock and my own talk with him at half past, I might be able to put two and two together without making five of it. So I made an appointment with her to have dinner with me later and to tell me how she got on with Zona."

Gaunt threw his cigarette-end into the fire and lit a fresh one.

"At seven o'clock," he went on, "Meralda telephoned me at my office. She said she'd killed Zona--shot him. And I can't say that I was fearfully surprised."

                                    Peter Cheyney

Ricket opened his eyes. "No?" he said. "And why not?"

"I'll tell you," said Gaunt. "When she was at my office earlier in the day, while she was telling me about the conversation she had had with Lorimer in which she had insisted that he should get out of London, she told me that he had given her a gun. She showed it to me. It was a 0.32 Colt automatic. She said that Lorimer had given her the gun because he was afraid of what Zona might get up to while he was away. He thought that possibly she might be in danger of her life.

"When she came round here, apparently she had a first-class row with Zona and as a result of that row he was shot."

Ricket fumbled in his overcoat pocket and produced a briar pipe and tobacco pouch. He began to fill the pipe.

"I like the way you put that last bit, Rufus," he said. "It's what might be called 'noncommittal.' You say they had a row and as a result of the row Zona was shot. That might mean anything."

"Exactly," said Gaunt. "If I had any more particulars I'd give them to you. But I agree with you it might mean anything. It might mean that Meralda Grey lost her temper, pulled out the gun and shot Zona. The second solution would be that Zona threatened her with a gun and she killed him in self-defence."

Ricket began to grin. "I think you're a bit ahead of me, Rufus," he said. "If this Meralda Grey woman fired in self-defence, where's the gun with which Zona threatened her? You haven't touched anything since you've been here, have you?"

"Not a thing," said Gaunt. "I wouldn't do a thing like that--you know that, Ricket. But if you go into the bedroom you'll find there is a double window leading out on to the fire-escape. You'll notice that it is closed but unlatched on the inside. Supposing she had shot Zona in self-defence, if somebody else had been in the apartment concealed in the bedroom, they could have come in after she'd gone and taken the gun out of Zona's hand and gone down by the fire escape."

"Very nice," said Ricket. "What are you trying to do--make out a case for this Miss Grey?" He grinned cynically. "She's not a friend of yours by any chance, is she?" he asked.

Gaunt smiled. "I never met her till last night," he said.

Ricket said: "I don't see why we should concern ourselves with all these surmises. You say she telephoned you and told you she'd shot Zona. I imagine that if she'd shot Zona in self-defence she'd have told you so. Did she?"

Gaunt held up his hand. "Now you can't expect

    Peter Cheyney

me to answer a question like that, Ricket," he said. "Even if I told you it wouldn't be any good as evidence. Presumably you'll have to take a statement from Miss Grey, and presumably she's going to tell you anything she wants to tell you. and I imagine that will be the truth."

"Where is she?" Ricket asked.

"I don't know," Gaunt lied glibly. "I've got an idea she was going off to see her mother who lives somewhere in the country, but I suppose she'll return to her flat some time or other. You'll find her easily enough."

"We'll find her all right," said Ricket. "You know, Rufus, I hate to disbelieve anything you say, although I've got an idea that your sympathies, if any, are with the Grey woman. I rather think that mine are too--I can quite understand anybody wanting to kill Zona. But that's purely a personal angle. As far as I can see from what I've heard from you this case is in the bag. It is a clear-cut case of murder."

Gaunt sat down in the armchair opposite Ricket. "Tell me the way you see it," he said.

"It looks perfectly simple to me," said Ricket. "Yesterday, things came to a head with Zona. Now both you and I know that Zona was pretty tough--that boy was no baby. He didn't frighten easily. If Zona was sufficiency scared to ring you up and ask you to go round and see him for the purpose of looking after him he was pretty good and frightened." He grinned. "He knew that Rufus Gaunt is one of the most expensive investigators in London. He knew that you'd want paying--and paying well--for anything you did, and I never heard that Mario Zona was a man to throw money about needlessly. So we can take it that there was some sort of a climax yesterday. On what you've told me, some sort of situation came to a head. The situation was between Zona, this fellow Lorimer who's his manager, who Zona said had been robbing him, and of whom Zona professes to be afraid, and Meralda Grey who is Lorimer's fiancée, who professes to be so afraid for Lorimer that she sends him out of the way. It is the eternal triangle of two men and one woman, with a little robbery thrown in.

"Naturally, the girl is concerned; she is concerned about Lorimer. The very fact that she sent him out of the way this morning proves that she was afraid for him. Now it looks to me as if the only reason why she would send him away was because she was afraid for his life. In other words Meralda Grey thought that there was a good chance of Zona killing Michael Lorimer.

"Quite obviously this thing played on the girl's nerves. I think its quite on the cards that when Lorimer went away he was afraid for the girl. He

　　　　　　　　　　　Peter Cheyney

would naturally be afraid. He'd feel that Zona would be angry because she'd persuaded him, Lorimer, to get out of the way."

Ricket tamped down the tobacco in his pipe with the end of a pencil that he produced from his waistcoat pocket. Then he re-lit it.

"Women are funny things," he said.

Gaunt said: "You always were a hell of a psychologist, Ricket."

Ricket grinned. "You're telling me," he said. "You private detectives think you've got all the brains. Well, after she'd seen you in your office she intended to have a show-down with Zona. She said she was going to have a show-down and what does that mean? A show-down means a settlement one way or another--doesn't it? Possibly she thought that she could get some sort of guarantee from Zona that he'd lay off Lorimer. Zona wasn't prepared to give it. More, he probably told her just what his ideas were about Lorimer, just what he was going to do.

"She didn't like it, so she brought the situation to a head by shooting Zona. In other words a plain simple clear-cut case of premeditated murder; premeditated because she had a gun in her hand-bag when she went round to see Zona."

Gaunt got up. Outside in the street he could hear the sound of another car pulling up. This would be the car containing the surgeon and the

Yard photographer. He turned round and walked back to the fireplace. He stood with his back to it, looking down at Ricket.

"I think that your solution of this business is first-class, Ricket," he said. "But there is just one little point that's going to upset it."

Ricket raise his eyebrows. "Oh yes," he said cynically. "And what's that?"

"After Meralda Grey telephoned me," said Gaunt quietly, "I saw her. I met her in a cocktail bar. We had a drink together. That was when she told me she was going off to her mother's place. She was in a pretty bad way."

"I'll bet she was," said Ricket. "I've never known a woman kill a man who wasn't in a bad way immediately afterwards."

Gaunt said, "That's all right, but the point is she didn't kill this man. I know she didn't."

Ricket got up. "Look here, Rufus," he said. "What do you mean? What are you playing at?"

"I'm not playing at anything," said Gaunt. "I'm just telling you what happened."

He put his hand in his overcoat pocket and produced the Colt automatic that he'd taken from Meralda Grey.

"Here's the gun that Meralda Grey had when she came round to see Zona," he said. "I asked her for it and she gave it to me while we were having that drink. You look at it. It is loaded with ten shells. One of them's been fired, but if you like to take out the cartridge clip and look at the shell cases, you'll see that every shell in that gun is blank ammunition. The gun was only loaded with blanks so she couldn't have killed Zona."

Ricket put out his hand and took the gun. He pulled out the ammunition clip, put the end of his thumb underneath the spring, pushed the shells out into 'his hand. He whistled.

"These are blanks all right," he said. He stood for a moment looking at the nine shells that lay in the palm of his left hand. Then he looked at Gaunt. "You say you only met Meralda Grey last night," he said. "Well, Rufus, I believe you, because I've got to. But you know what I'm thinking?"

Gaunt grinned. "I haven't got enough brains," he said. "You tell me what you're thinking."

Ricket said: "You've had this gun in your possession for nearly an hour. If you wanted to, you had lots of time to take out the ball ammunition and replace it with blank."

Gaunt continued to grin. "You don't say, Ricket," he said. "Well that's just a surmise on your part. You prove it."

V. -- GERALDINE

IT was ten minutes past nine when Gaunt left the Colindale Apartments and walked in the direction of Bond Street. He went into the telephone box at the corner of Brook Street, looked up Meralda Grey's number. He got through to her on the telephone.

"This is Gaunt speaking," he said when he heard her voice on the line. "I want you to listen very carefully to what I have to say, and I've no time for long explanations. First of all, you didn't kill Zona. Do you understand that? You only think you did. You fired at him all right, but you didn't kill him. You didn't kill Zona because the ammunition in that automatic pistol of yours was blank."

He heard her gasp. "But...." she began.

"But nothing," said Gaunt. "I tell you the ammunition was blank. I've just left Zona's apartment. Detective-Inspector Ricket from the Yard is round there now. Some time soon he is going to see you and get a statement from you, but he won't worry about you for a while because I've told him you've gone to your mother's.

"What I want you to do immediately is to pack a bag, take a cab and go to the Cygnet Hotel in Bedford Square. Register there as Miss Stevenson of

Glasgow. I want you to stay there for a day or two. I'll produce you for Ricket when the time's right. And don't go to the Silver Ring tonight. By the way, who'll be running that place now?

"Wolfe Lanel--Zona's secretary. He'll be looking after the place. But I don't understand..."

"I don't expect you do," said Gaunt, "but if you do what I tell you I think I can get you out of this. If you don't it won't be so good for you. Are you going to obey orders?"

"I don't see what else I can do," she said. "I can't even think. I'm frightened."

"You bet you're frightened," said Gaunt. "Now you pack and get round to the Cygnet. Don't forget you're Miss Stevenson--Mary Stevenson--from Glasgow. I'll come round and see you some time."

"Very well," she said. "I'll do what you say."

Gaunt hung up.

He walked across Bond Street, through Hanover Square to The Silver Ring Club. When he got there the place was just beginning to fill up. He sat down at a table and ordered a whisky and soda. He felt in his pocket for a cigarette, found he hadn't one, signalled to the cigarette-girl who stood with her tray on the other side of the balcony.

She came over. Gaunt thought she was a good-looking little thing. She was short, blonde and pretty, with an exceptional figure. Gaunt noticed that her shoes and stockings were expensive, much too expensive for a cigarette-girl in a night club.

The detective took a box of cigarettes from the tray. Looking at the girl, he saw that her face was pale and the hand that held the tray was trembling. A sudden idea came to him.

He said: "What's your name, my dear?" He looked at her smilingly.

"My name's Nellie Winter," she said. "But everybody calls me Geraldine."

"All right, Geraldine," said Gaunt. "Now you tell me something. When did you see Mr. Zona last?"

She looked at him. He noticed the sudden sag of her jaw.

"So you know about it?" he said. "Isn't that right, Geraldine?"

She tossed her head. "I don't know what you're talking about," she said.

But Gaunt could see that her lips were trembling. He tried another shot.

"Where were you this evening about seven o'clock?" he asked.

She looked him straight in the eye, "I'm not going to answer your questions," she said. "Why should I?"

She turned on her heel and walked away. Gaunt got up and walked back to the cloakroom. There were two telephones on a shelf behind the barrier.

Gaunt said to the girl in charge: "I had an appointment with Mr. Zona to see him at his apartment round about seven o'clock tonight, My name's Gaunt. I'm a detective. I'm investigating some business for him. He didn't by any chance come through on the telephone and leave a message for me?"

"No, sir," said the girl. "He telephoned through about six-thirty, but he didn't say anything about you."

Gaunt said: "What did he telephone through for?" He pushed a pound note across the counter towards her.

She said: "He said I was to tell Geraldine if she was here that she was to hurry."

"Thanks," said Gaunt."

He walked back into the main room round the right hand balcony, through the pass door and tapped on the door of Zona's office. Somebody said "Come in." He went in.

A man was sitting behind Zona's desk working on some papers. He was about forty-five years of age, thick-set, intelligent-looking.,

Gaunt said: "Are you Wolfe Lanel--Zona's secretary?"

Lanel smiled. "Yes, I am," he said. "I suppose you're Mr. Gaunt. Zona spoke to me about you."

"That's fine," said Gaunt. "Well, Lanel, listen

to this: Zona was shot tonight. Somebody went round to his apartment and killed him. The police are round there now.

He felt In his pocket for a cigarette, found he hadn't one, signalled to the cigarette girl.

"I think before they're through on this job, there's going to be considerable trouble for a lot of people. I hope it won't include you."

Lanel put down his fountain-pen. He was quite unperturbed.

He said: "Between you and me and the door-post, Mr. Gaunt, I think. Zona had it coming to him."

"You don't say," said Gaunt. "Didn't you like him?"

Lanel shrugged his shoulders. "I worked for him," he said. "I didn't have to like him. To tell you the truth I never met anybody who did."

Gaunt opened his new packet of cigarettes. He offered one to Lanel, took one himself.

"Between you and me, Lanel," he said. "Why was it that Zona was so unpopular?"

Lanel smiled cynically. Gaunt had a momentary glimpse of a set of very strong white teeth

"Women," said Lanel. "He had an idea that every woman who worked for him had got to fall for him."

"I know," said Gaunt. "There are a lot of night

                                        Peter Cheyney

club proprietors like that." He blew a smoke ring into the air. "I bet he made things pretty tough for that kid, Geraldine. She's a pretty girl too."

He noticed the spasmodic movement of Lanel's fingers as he mentioned the girl's name.

Lanel said: "If it isn't impertinent, Mr. Gaunt, just what angle are you working on now? I understood from Zona yesterday that you were coming in to do an investigation about the accounts discrepancies."

"That still goes," said Gaunt. "You see, Zona paid me my fee last night and when I'm paid I like to do my job. Incidentally, if you're going to run this club I might save you some trouble... and Geraldine."

Lanel looked up. His eyes were hostile. "There's no need to bring her into this," he said. "That girl's a good kid. Everybody likes her. Why should she be mentioned in connection with Zona being killed?"

Gaunt sent a stream of cigarette smoke out of his nostrils. "There is every reason," he said. "Didn't you know that she had an appointment with Zona tonight?"

"I didn't," said Lanel. "And neither do you."

Gaunt grinned. "Oh, yes, I do," he said. "I just bought some cigarettes from her. I noticed that she looked, scared stiff. So I asked her when she saw Zona last. She didn't have to answer. I saw the effect that the question had on her. Just to make sure I went out and had a word with the girl in the cloakroom--the girl who answers the telephones here. Apparently Zona came through here about six-thirty and left a message that Geraldine was to hurry. That tells me all I want to know."

Lanel began to speak, but Gaunt put up his hand and stopped him.

"I'm not suggesting anything," he said, "and you needn't begin to worry, Lanel, even if you are a bit keen on Geraldine yourself." His grin deepened. "It doesn't mean, because she went round there, that she killed Zona, but it does mean that everybody who was round there about that time is going to be suspect. Why did she go round to see Zona?"

Lanel got up. He began to walk up and down the office. "Look here, Mr. Gaunt," he said, "I'd like to play straight with you. I suppose everything will have to come out some time." He spun round. "I'll tell you the truth," he said. "I'm damned glad Zona's dead, and everybody else at this place will be glad too. Zona was poison."

Gaunt nodded. "I rather thought that myself," he said. "But even a man who's poison is entitled not to be murdered."

"Geraldine went round there this evening be-cause I told her to go there and tell Zona where he got off once and for all," said Lanel. He stubbed out his half-smoked cigarette in the ash-tray on the desk.

Peter Cheyney

"He's been making that kid's life a misery for months," he said. "She's a nice girl, Mr. Gaunt. She's twenty-four. I've always had an idea in my head that there was some funny business going on in this place upstairs after we'd closed down officially at night. There's no doubt in my mind that Zona was trying to get Geraldine to take some part in it. Just what was going on, just what he wanted her to do, I don't know. She wouldn't tell me.

"Late this afternoon, when I was round here, she came into the club. She told me about it. She's always sort of liked me," he said diffidently. "But she was being very careful about what she said, and the reason wasn't far to seek. Like everybody else she was scared of Zona. Possibly he'd got something on her, or bluffed her that he had.

"I said that the best thing that she could do would be to go round and see Zona and tell him that she'd told me about it; that he'd got to lay off her. I advised her merely to ring through to Zona and say she'd like to see him, not to mention what the conversation was to be about. She did that. She telephoned through from here. Zona told her to get round there at about a quarter past six. But apparently, if what you say is right, she didn't get there on time. He sent that message through at half past six, to tell her to hurry, after she'd left."

Gaunt lit another cigarette. "Very interesting,"

he said. "Now tell me something else, Lanel. You knew Zona pretty well and I imagine you know the people who worked for him. Who do you think would be the person who'd want Zona out of the way most of all? If he hadn't been killed and you were reviewing a list of all the people who'd like to kill him, who would you put at the top?"

Lanel thought for a moment. Then he said: "You probably won't believe what I am going to say, but I'd have put Zona at the top of the list."

Gaunt raised one eyebrow. "Zona? What do you mean?"

Lanel put his elbows on the desk and looked at Gaunt.

"I think Zona was ripe for committing suicide," he said. "During the last month I've heard him say, not once but a dozen times, that he was sick of the whole business, that he was sick of life, and that for two pins he'd finish it. He had good reason, too," he went on. "He's had trouble with money, trouble with women, trouble everywhere. Two weeks ago he had a fainting fit here in the office. He went to a doctor--who found his heart was in a bad way. I don't think Zona had very long to live anyway."

He picked up a pencil and began drawing lines on the blotting paper in front of him. "It's a funny thing," he said, "when you came in and said that someone had shot Zona, the first thought that come in my head was 'suicide.'"

Gaunt said nothing. He sat there smoking silently, thinking. Lanel got up again, began to walk about restlessly.

"Zona's been fearfully odd lately," he went on. "Very secretive. I've known most of his business for the last two years, but during the last month he's been as tight as a clam. I used to go round to his place at the Colindale Apartments practically every afternoon to discuss the previous day's takings, and to take any special instructions he had to give. Once or twice when I've been round there lately the outer door of the flat's been locked and though I've rung the bell, and although I could hear somebody moving about inside, nobody answered.

"Three days ago when I was there, there was an odd noise coming from the flat, a peculiar noise rather like the noise of somebody sawing wood. The day before yesterday, when Zona was to the office, he sent me round to his apartment for some papers. He gave me a key, an extra one he used to keep here. I forgot to give it back to him. Yesterday I went there in the afternoon to return the documents I'd brought away. I didn't ring the bell; I opened the door with the key and went straight in.

"I went into the study. All the books had been pulled down from the bookshelves and were lying higgledy-piggledy over the floor. The edges of the carpet had been turned up and the place looked as if a battle had been going on. When I got back I mentioned the untidiness of the apartment to Zona. He told me to mind my own damn business."

Gaunt got up. "Thank you, Lanel," he said. "I think you've been very frank."

His face was smiling, although behind it his mind was wondering about Wolfe Lanel. The idea occurred to Gaunt that Lanel had taken the news of Zona's murder very quietly, almost, too quietly.

"I'll be seeing you again," said Gaunt, and walked out of the office.

HE got his hat at the cloakroom, picked up the telephone, dialled Scotland Yard and asked if Detective-Inspector Ricket had returned yet, if so whether he could speak on the phone.

After a minute Ricket came on the line..

"Listen, Ricket," said Gaunt. "Will you do me a favour? I want to have a look around Zona's apartment. It might be a help to you, and I don't want to get in the same way as I did last time."

"I'm glad of that," said Ricket. "I was wondering how you got that door open. All right, Gaunt, if you want to have a look you can. You'll find a man on duty downstairs with the hall porter. I'll phone through an instruction that you're to be admitted. By the way, I'd like a statement from you tomorrow, and I want one from that girl Meralda Grey, too. We cant find her. She's not at her flat."

"She'll turn up," said Gaunt, "and I'll see you tomorrow about that statement. Maybe it'll be more interesting than you know."

VI. -- Set-up for Suicide

IT was ten-thirty when Gaunt arrived at the Colindale Apartments. He showed his visiting card to the police officer who was on duty downstairs and went straight up to Zona's apartment.

Alone in the study, from which the body of the night club proprietor had been removed, Gaunt lit a cigarette, sat down before the dead fire and indulged in some quiet thought.

His recent conversation with Wolfe Lanel had produced some new and possibly startling angles in his mind. He was particularly interested in the information which Lanel had given him concerning his recent visits to the flat. He was intrigued by the fact that Lanel had gone out of his way to tell him of the untidiness of the flat on his last visit, and the story about the books taken from the bookshelves lying about the floor. Such a process was not uncommon. Bookshelves had to be dusted sometimes.

He walked over to the bookshelves which ran the whole length of the wall on the right hand side of the room and examined the books closely. It was obvious that those at the left hand side of the shelves had been untouched, for there was a thin layer of dust along the edges of the shelves. But at the right hand side of two shelves--the ones nearest

Peter Cheyney

Zona's desk--the books had obviously been recently moved.

Gaunt began to take them out, stacking them in piles on the floor. When he had moved the books at the right-hand end of the third shelf he saw, fitted at the back of the bookcase, let into the wall, a small sliding panel. It opened quite easily. Behind the panel was a box-like aperture.

Gaunt struck a match and examined it. It was empty. He closed the panel and replaced the books. He thought it rather odd that if the books had been removed when Lanel had visited the flat, he had not seen the sliding panel. It would be impossible not to see it. Gaunt permitted himself a grin. It looked as if there was method in Lanel's line of information.

So much for the books. The other point which Lanel had been careful to stress was the fact that the carpet had been turned up. Gaunt looked down at the square of black-edged fawn carpet on which Zona's desk stood. He went behind the desk and examined the edges of the carpet. They were securely tacked down, but under the desk itself about the spot where the feet of a person sitting at the desk would rest, he noticed a rather odd looseness on the surface of the carpet. He pushed aside the chair, knelt down and stuck a match. He gave a whistle of surprise. Along the right hand side of the desk-well, hidden in the shadow, the carpet had been cut for a good twelve inches. The detective caught hold of the cut edge, pulled it back. Underneath an eighteen inch square in the flooring beneath the desk had been cut away.

Gaunt threw away the match end and struck another. Here was the explanation of the sawing noise that Lanel had heard. Gaunt put his hand down into the aperture. Withdrawing it his fingers caught on a tiny projection sticking out from the cut side of the floorboard. He bent closer and examined it. It was a nail head. Caught over the nail head was a piece of string.

Gaunt put his finger underneath and pulled. Obviously, there was a weight on the end of the string. He gripped the string firmly, pulled it up. Three or four feet of double string came up and Gaunt's eyes glistened as he saw the objects tied to the two ends. On one end of the string was an automatic pistol, on the other end a paper-weight.

Gaunt put the articles on the desk, pulled hack the chair, sat down and examined them. The pistol was a 0.32 Colt automatic, a weapon of exactly the same type as that which Meralda Grey had carried. Gaunt, handling the gun with his handkerchief, pulled out the ammunition clip and examined it. There were nine cartridge in the clip--the tenth was missing. Gaunt remembered that he had found one empty shell on the carpet during his visit after hearing the news of Zona's death from Meralda. He wondered which gun the shell had come from? Had it come from her gun--for the shell of a discharged blank cartridge was the same as that of a discharged live one--or had it come from the gun in his hand?

He got up from the desk, walked across the room and sat down once more by the fireplace. Here was a possible explanation of Lanel's theory about Zona being a would-be suicide. The whole set-up was perfectly obvious. An Individual wishing to commit suicide could have sat at that desk holding in his hand an automatic with which he intended to shoot himself. Tied to the butt end of the automatic was a piece of string with a paper-weight fixed to the other end. The paper weight would be already pushed through the hole cut in the floorboards beneath the desk. When the pistol was fired it would drop from the hand that had pressed the trigger, the weight on the end of the string would pull it through the slit in the carpet, through the hole in the floor-boards beneath, The carpet, made of strong fibre, would automatically spring back into its place, and the weapon with which the suicide had been committed would disappear. Only the dead man would remain.

Gaunt's lips curved into a cynical smile as he realised that the set-up was just as perfect for murder as for an actual suicide. A clever murderer might evolve such a plan.

All that he would have to do would be to slit the carpet and cut the hole in the floorboards at a time when Zona was away. It would be quite easy to tie on the string and the paper-weight after the murder had been committed. Gaunt realised that had it not been for the nail-head sticking out in the side of the floor-board on which the string had caught as the pistol fell the gun would probably never have been found. He realised, too, the explanation of the aperture behind the bookshelves. This was the place where Zona had kept the gun.

Gaunt began to think about Lanel. Lanel had had the key to Zona's flat. He had had ample opportunity to go round to the flat, to remove the floorboards himself, to prepare the whole set-up in case he should want it. Lanel probably knew where Zona kept his gun.

Was Lanel the murderer and had he told Gaunt about the noise of sawing, the books on the floor, his inability to get into the flat, merely to concentrate the detective's attention on these points, merely to lead him to the pistol and the string and the paper-weight which he, Lanel, had carefully and deliberately hung over the nail so that Gaunt should find it?

If this were so, the idea in Lanel's mind was obvious. He wanted Gaunt to believe that Zona had prepared this little scheme; that Zona, fed up with life, had decided to put an end to it, but in ending it had also decided that, by arranging the disappearance of the suicide pistol, suspicion of murder should fall on someone else. Who would that someone be? Surely the last person to be in the flat before his dead body was discovered. That last person, excluding Gaunt, would be Meralda Grey who was to see Zona at seven o'clock. Had Zona made the appointment with Gaunt for seven-thirty in order that the detective should discover his dead body; that he should suspect Meralda Grey? Had Zona planned to bid farewell to a world of which he was heartily sick and in doing so to plan a terrible vengeance on Michael Lorimer and the girl, both of whom would be suspect? Or had Lanel plotted the whole scheme and very nearly carried it through to a successful conclusion?

There was one snag to this theory. Lanel knew that Geraldine was going round to see Zona early that evening. He knew she was going round because he himself had advised her to go round. Unless therefore Lanel knew that somebody was going to see Zona after Geraldine had visited him he would automatically be throwing suspicion on the cigarette-girl.

Gaunt lit another cigarette and pondered on the jigsaw puzzle that was now presenting itself.

His mind went back to his interview that evening with Meralda Grey at the Laurel Restaurant after the death of Zona had occurred. She had told him that Zona had sent her round a note telling her not to come round and see him. At first thought the dispatching of this note would indicate that Zona could have not plot in his mind against Meralda, inasmuch as if she did not go to the flat she could not be suspected of having killed him, but Meralda had also said that the note itself was insulting, that it made further accusations against her.

Had Zona written that note knowing Meralda's temper, knowing that its receipt would automatically ensure her presence at the flat in order to demand an explanation?

Gaunt realised that the note from Zona was neither a help nor a hindrance. It meant nothing at all.

He switched his mind to Ricket. Here, at least, was one bright spot in the business. Gaunt realised that, had it not been for the fact that he had informed the Detective-Inspector that Meralda Grey had said that she had killed Zona, Ricket would have searched the entire flat with a metaphorical toothcomb, looking for some clue that would lead him to a possible murderer. Ricket would have found the slit in the carpet beneath the desk, the sawn-away floorboards, the string, the pistol and the paper-weight. Ricket would have immediately

Peter Cheyney

suspected suicide. Well... Why should not Ricket still suspect suicide?

Gaunt allowed his mind to wander. One thing was certain. Whoever had arranged the suicide scenario, whoever had organised it so carefully, had done so before Zona died. There would have been no time afterwards. Zona was alive at seven o'clock when Meralda Grey went round to see him. Meralda Grey thought that she had shot him, but Gaunt thought he knew the explanation of that.

Was it possible that it was Zona himself who had rigged up this grotesque apparatus of death, and used it? At the moment, to Gaunt's way of thinking, two people could have arranged the suicide picture, one was Zona, the other Lanel.

And there was possibly a third suspect. What about Geraldine? If what Lanel had said was true it was more than possible that Geraldine had visited the flat on previous occasions; it was possible that Zona might have given her a key. And her attitude had been strange when Gaunt had talked to her at The Silver Ring. Everything about the girl had seemed to indicate that she knew then that Zona was dead; that she did not want to discuss what had happened.

Gaunt threw his cigarette stub into the grate and began to walk about the room. In any event the new evidence would give Ricket something to think about. Gaunt grinned at the thought that Ricket would have to believe his story now, would have to believe that the automatic pistol that Meralda Grey had fired at Zona was loaded with blank cartridges. Gaunt saw just how he could make Ricket believe that.

Almost at the same moment he wondered why he was taking all this trouble. He had already made a good profit on the Zona "investigation." There was no real reason why he should continue to investigate something which was a concern of the police and nothing to do with him. Yet at the back of his mind he knew there was a reason--Meralda Grey.

The idea came to him that he was allowing himself to become much too interested in that young woman from a personal angle. Gaunt had met many women, had liked some of them, but there was something about Meralda Grey which appealed to him, something very definitely attractive.

He began to think about Michael Lorimer. Whoever he was, and wherever he was, Gaunt thought that the young man ought to consider himself lucky to be engaged to a girl like Meralda. He wondered what Lorimer would think, what he would do, when, next day, he read the news of Zona's death in the newspapers--or as much of it as the enterprising Ricket had decided to release for publication.

                    Peter Cheyney

But Ricket would probably do nothing until next morning. He would concentrate on finding Meralda Grey. He would do that because he would be sure--of this Gaunt was certain--that she had killed Zona, and that he, Gaunt, for some reason best known to himself had, after Zona had been killed, deliberately removed the live cartridges from the gun and reloaded it with blanks.

The detective shrugged his shoulders. Then he walked over to the desk, took off the telephone and rang through to Ricket at Scotland Yard

After a moment ne heard Ricket's voice on the line.

"Listen, Ricket," said Gaunt evenly. "I'm speaking to you from Zona's flat. I've just found some very interesting evidence. Zona wasn't murdered."

"You don't say!" said Ricket. "You're getting some bright ideas today, aren't you, Gaunt? This is one of the nicest murder cases I've ever been on. First of all a young woman rings you up and tells you that she has killed Zona. Then you make the amazing discovery that the pistol with which she shot Zona was loaded with blank ammunition, and now you tell me that he wasn't murdered at all. I suppose the next thing you'll be telling me is that he is alive; that the body we took away from the Colindale Apartments didn't even exist?"

Gaunt laughed. "Zona's dead all right. I said he

wasn't murdered. If you like to come round here I'll prove it to you."

"I see," said Ricket. "Well... you'll have to prove it. Somebody's going to tell me that this job was done by Father Christmas in a minute. By the way, you haven't any idea as to the exact whereabouts of Miss Meralda Grey at this moment, have you? And I don't want to get funny with you, Rufus, but you know there is a law against obstruction of a police officer in the execution of his duty. I believe you've got that young woman hidden away somewhere. What about it?"

"I wouldn't do a thing like that, Ricket," said Gaunt. He was grinning. "You'll be able to see Miss Grey any time you want to."

"I see," said Ricket. "Now would you mind telling me just what did happen to Zona?"

"Certainly," said Gaunt. "Zona committed suicide."

VII. -- Motive for Murder

IT was midnight when Gaunt went into the telephone box at the corner of Brook Street and rang through to the Cygnet Hotel. He asked to speak to Miss Mary Stevenson. Whilst he waited for the call to be put through he lit a cigarette and congratulated himself on the fact that Ricket's mind was now definitely unsettled on his original theory as to Zona's killer; that he was seriously prepared to consider the possibilities of suicide.

When Meralda Grey came on the line he said: "How are you, Miss Stevenson? I'm just going round to my office in Conduit Street. I thought you might like to get into a cab and come along. I know it's very late but the business is important."

"Very well," she said, I'll come round at once."

Gaunt , hung up, walked back to the office. He let himself in, switched on the lights and left the outer office door open. He sat down at his desk, deep in thought.

A quarter of an hour afterwards Gaunt heard the downstairs door close softly. He walked through into the outer office and waited for Meralda. As she came out of the darkness of the passage into the well-lit room, he noticed the fear and worry In her eyes, the droop of her shoulders, He closed the door and motioned her towards the inner office.

"You sit down in that big chair and relax," he said. "And you can relax because although you're not entirely out of the wood yet I think you're fairly safe. I think we've managed to upset the theory that you shot Zona."

She said hopelessly: "But I did shoot him. I'm certain I did."

"You can set your mind at rest," said Gaunt. "I say you didn't. Even Ricket--the Detective-Inspector in charge of the case--is beginning to believe that."

He handed her a cigarette and lit it.

"This is what happened," he said. "According to your story, when you fired at Zona he was sitting at his desk. You were standing on the right of the desk. You fired at him. You told me that you saw a red mark appear on the side of his head. That would be the left-hand side. Then you saw him slump forward. After that you turned and hurried out of the place.

"My theory is that if you'd stayed for five or six minutes you'd have seen Zona pull himself together and sit back in the chair."

He inhaled deeply, blowing the smoke slowly through his nostrils.

"Our story is that when you pressed the. trigger of that automatic," he said, "you fired a blank

                                    Peter Cheyney

cartridge. The wad out of that cartridge hit Zona on the left-hand side of the head. Naturally it made a mark. Also it half stunned him temporarily. That wad was fired at a range of about six feet--it could easily knock a man out.

"The next point is this: The bullet that actually killed Zona was fired from the other side of the desk. It entered through the right-hand side of the head just behind the temple and came out on the left-hand side of the neck. Ricket can't find that bullet. The reason he can't find it is that the murderer or murderess"--Gaunt stressed the word--"searched for it, found it and took it away."

She nodded. Then gave a sigh--a sigh of relief.

"How wonderful," she said, "to think that I didn't kill Zona. I've realised since that there was no possible excuse for what I did, except that I honestly and truly didn't know what I was doing."

"I can believe that," said Gaunt, "You were in such a rage that you acted almost subconsciously. But you're not out of the wood yet. You've got to remember that you were one of the people who went up to see Zona. You'll be a suspect. After all somebody shot him, although at the moment Ricket is inclined to believe that there is more than a possibility that he shot himself."

"Why?" she asked in amazement.

Gaunt told her of his discovery of the second

automatic pistol--the one which he had found hanging from a nail in the floorboards.

"This suicide theory is a little bit far-fetched," he said. "Let's consider it. If Zona meant to commit suicide, and to do it in such a way that suspicion was going to fall on you, he would have to know first of all that you were coming round to his flat at the right time; secondly, that you were going to bring a pistol with you.

"Not only would he have to be certain of that, but he would also have to know the type of pistol you were going to use, and its calibre. The bullet would have to be of the same size and type. Of course, one might say that he need not have to know any of these things; that providing he had his fake apparatus rigged up, you would be suspect in any event. And that if you actually had no pistol when you went round to see him the police theory would be that you had taken a gun in with you and got rid of it after the murder."

She nodded.

Gaunt blew a smoke ring.

"There might be another theory," he said. "A more plausible theory, I've mentioned it to nobody; it is my own idea."

She leant forward. "What is it, Mr. Gaunt?" she asked.

"Let's take it for the sake of argument," said

Gaunt, "that the fact that the second pistol was a 0.32 Colt automatic was not a coincidence; that whoever put it where I found it had some definite idea of putting a gun of that type there. Can you think of a possible reason why that type of gun should be used?"

She shook her head. "No, I can't," she said. "Can there be one?"

He grinned at her. "A very good one, Miss Grey," he said. "Cast your mind back. Who gave you the gun that you had in your handbag when you went round to see Zona?"

"Why, Michael did of course," she said. "But--"

"Well, don't you see?" said Gaunt. "Mightn't it be that whoever it was rigged up that apparatus knew that Michael possessed a 0.32 Colt automatic? Doesn't it look as if the idea was that suspicion should fall on him? Don't you see that if someone knew that Michael had a 0.32 Colt and rigged up that apparatus with the idea that it would he discovered, they would know that the fact that Michael had a 0.32 gun would automatically bring suspicion on him?"

"I see," she said. "But if someone were plotting for Michael to be suspected of murdering Zona, how would they know that the police would have found what you found. After all, the police didn't find it, did they?"

"Precisely," said Gaunt. "But the only reason they didn't find it was they didn't look for it, and the only reason they didn't search the flat with a fine-tooth-comb was because I told them that the murderer--yourself--had already confessed. They thought there wasn't any necessity to look.

"It might very easily be that the person desiring suspicion to fall on Michael had an idea that Michael was going round to see Zona, not you. Then they would reason this way. If Michael had been round to the flat and afterwards Zona was discovered dead, suspicion would automatically fall on him whether they found the concealed weapon or not. The police would know that there had been trouble between Michael and Zona. My evidence would prove that because Zona had told me that he suspected Michael. Even if they didn't find the second gun, Michael would have a lot of trouble to clear himself of the charge.

"If they did find the second gun they might consider possibly that Zona had committed suicide. But there is one very good factor mitigating against that theory. The bullet that killed Zona--the one that entered his head and came out of his neck--should be somewhere in that flat."

"I see," she said. "So it means that it was murder. Somebody did murder Zona. But I thought you said that the police think there was a possibility of suicide?"

"They do," said Gaunt. "But only for one reason."

He looked at her. He was smiling cynically.

"What is it?" she said.

"There is a way in which Zona could have committed suicide, and the bullet not have been found," said Gaunt. "If Zona had been standing up with his back to the desk, the obvious position if he had intended the suicide weapon to disappear through the slit in the carpet, on his left would have been the end of the bookcase and the window, which was open at the bottom. Having regard to the course which the bullet took it might easily have gone through the window, after which Zona in falling might have half turned and been in the position in which I found him.

"In that case," she said, "he would presumably have been lying on the right hand side of the desk facing it, probably lying on his side."

"No," said Gaunt. "He was huddled up in a peculiar grotesque position.

However," he said with a grin, "I got over that by telling Ricket that when I walked round the desk I touched his knees accidentally with my foot and he turned over."

She looked at him in amazement.

"Why did you do that?" she said. Are you trying

to shield someone?"

Gaunt grinned. "I don't know about that," he said. "I think if I'm trying to shield anybody its you." His grin broadened into a smile.

"Anyway," he went on, "Ricket's half satisfied that Zona who, according to Lanel, was fed up with life and everything in general, and with Michael Lorimer and yourself in particular--might have plotted, with that peculiarly cunning brain of his, this whole setup so that suspicion would fall on Michael. I hope he's going to continue thinking that."

"I see," she said. "And what do you want me to do now? I don't like staying at the Cygnet Hotel under a false name. I feel I'm running away,"

"There is no need for you to go on staying there," said Gaunt. "The way that Ricket's thinking at the moment will preclude him from arresting anybody. Tomorrow morning the papers will print the story of Zona's death. There'll be a coroner's inquest. But Ricket will get an adjournment in order to give him time to make further inquiries. Well, that's not going to be an easy process for him."

"Tomorrow morning you might as well go back to your own flat and resume your normal life. I shall be seeing Lanel. I'll tell him you'll be appearing tomorrow night at The Silver Ring. Just go on as if nothing had happened."

"Very well," she said. "I'll do that. You're very

mysterious, aren't you?"

"Am I?" said Gaunt. "Why?"

She got up, stubbed out her cigarette in the ashtray. She stood looking down at Gaunt as he sat in his chair by the desk. "You said just now," she went on, "that it wouldn't be particularly easy for Detective Inspector Ricket to make his inquiries. Why won't it be? Are you going to do something to make it more difficult?"

Gaunt grinned. "Why should I do that?" he said.

She passed her hand wearily across her forehead. "I don't know," she said. "Except that you seem the strangest sort of man. You do the strangest things. I'm still wondering why you were so keen on looking after me, in trying to remove suspicion from my shoulders at a time when I myself thought I'd killed Zona."

Gaunt lit another cigarette. His smile was more cynical than ever.

"There are always very good motives for anything I do, Miss Grey," he said. "And if you want to know why it won't be easy for Ricket to make his inquiries, I'll tell you. If Ricket knew the truth he'd have a great deal to worry about. You weren't the only person who went round tonight to see Zona at his apartment."

Her eyes widened. "No?" she said. "Who else went there?"

"Geraldine, the cigarette-girl at the club, for one," said Gaunt still grinning. "She went round there. Zona telephoned through to The Silver Ring Club at six-thirty and left a message that she was to hurry.

"If she'd gone straight round there and gone in by the main entrance, she might have arrived and left before you came on the scene. But she didn't do that. Only one person was seen to go into the entrance of the Colindale Apartments and up to Zona's flat tonight, and that was you."

She said: "But I don't understand. If Geraldine went round there and didn't go in the front entrance, how could she have seen Zona?"

"She went up the fire-escape," said Gaunt.

"I see," she said. "But why?"

"Work it out for yourself," the detective went on. "Lanel tells me that Zona had been making Geraldine's life a misery. Well, what does that mean? You know what sort of a man Zona was. He wouldn't want the hall porter and servants at the Colindale Apartments to know that he was being visited by one of the cigarette-girls from his own club. He would arrange for Geraldine to use the fire-escape."

She nodded her head. "You think of everything," she said. "Poor Geraldine. You don't think she could have done this, Mr. Gaunt, surely? She seems such a child."

Gaunt smiled again. "Anything can happen," he said. "You ought to know that. You, who a few hours ago thought that you yourself had killed a man! If you could do it, why shouldn't Geraldine? But because she used the fire-escape it doesn't mean to say that she did it. Maybe somebody else knew about that fire-escape.

"Who else?" she said.

"Lanel," said Gaunt. "A blind man could see that he's keen on Geraldine. It was he who advised the girl to go round tonight and settle things once and for all with Zona. It is rather peculiar that Zona should have to telephone through to the club and complain because the girl hadn't got round there although she had an appointment. It may be that Geraldine never went round there. It may be that she's merely afraid to say she didn't go round there because she knows that somebody else did."

"I see," said Meralda Grey. "You mean that..."

"I mean that Lanel told Geraldine to make an appointment with Zona in order to ensure Zona's presence in the flat; that he told Geraldine not to keep the appointment; that he went round himself; that he went up by the fire-escape, and that he shot Zona."

VIII. -- The Deal

IT was one-thirty when Gaunt arrived at The Silver Ring Club. He pushed aside the heavy velvet curtains that shielded the entrance, stepped on to the floor and stood for a moment watching the crowd of bored, well-dressed men and women who circulated to the soft strains of the latest "hot" number.

He stood there smoking a cigarette, looking around for Geraldine. He could not see her. After a moment he walked round the balcony and through the pass-door, he tapped on the door of the office and went in.

Lanel was sitting behind the desk at work on some accounts. Gaunt, looking at the secretary, thought that if Lanel was a murderer he had a good nerve; that he took things very quietly.

He said: "You look as if you're doing good business here, Lanel. Zona's absence doesn't seem to affect your customers very much."

The secretary shrugged his shoulders. "They don't know anything about it," he said. "When they do, they'll come here all the more. They're the sort of people who'd like to dance in a place where the proprietor has just been shot."

Gaunt nodded. He lit a cigarette, drew up a chair, sat down facing Lanel.

Peter Cheyney

"Where's Geraldine?" he asked.

"I sent her home," said Lanel, "She's upset. I had a talk with her. I told her what you said. How do you expect she feels?" He looked at Gaunt challengingly.

Gaunt said: "What else has been happening round here?"

Lanel laid down his fountain-pen. He took a cigarette from the box on the table, lit it and leant back in his chair.

"There's quite a lot been happening," he said. "First of all a Detective-Inspector Ricket has been round here. He's been asking a lot of questions." He looked straight at Gaunt. "He seemed to have the idea in his head that our star cabaret performer--Meralda--killed Zona. He seemed to be interested in you, too; he was asking how long you'd known her."

Gaunt grinned. "What else did he want to know?"

"He was interested in whether Zona had made a will or not. I told him he had. It's here in the office."

"Ah!" said Gaunt. "Now that is interesting. Who did Zona leave his money to?"

"Most of it goes to Meralda Grey," said Lanel. "Zona told me he was going to make another will," --he smiled cynically--"but it looks as if he didn't have time to do that."

"I see," said Gaunt. "That's nice for Meralda. Did Ricket have anything else to say?"

"Yes," said Lanel. "He was quite open about things. He said that Meralda thought she'd killed Zona, and that some time afterwards you discovered she couldn't have done that because the automatic pistol she used was loaded with blank cartridges." His grin deepened.

"And don't you believe that?" asked Gaunt.

Lanel shrugged his shoulders.

Gaunt said: "You listen to me. Lanel, and don't make any mistakes either. I'm a nasty fellow to get up against. If I say that the gun was loaded with blank ammunition, you're going to believe it and like it. You understand that, otherwise..."

"Otherwise what?" Lanel asked.

Gaunt examined the glowing end of his cigarette.

"Meralda Grey wasn't the only person to see Zona about the time he was killed. Your girl friend--" he held up his hand--"there's no need for you to argue, Lanel; anybody could see she is your girl friend--Geraldine was round there too, and in much more suspicious circumstances than the Grey woman."

"Really," said Lanel. "And how do you make that out?"

"The hall porter at the Colindale Apartments," Gaunt went on, "was on duty in the hall during the operative times. At least Meralda Grey had the honesty to go in by the front way. Geraldine didn't. She went in by the way she's used to going in--by the fire-escape."

"That's a damn lie," said Lanel.

Gaunt shrugged his shoulders. "Maybe," he said. "But the girl out there in the phone box can prove that at half past six Zona phoned through to tell Geraldine to hurry. I don't believe she went round there till after seven o'clock if she went at all."

"What do you mean by that?" asked Lanel. "if she went at all... I thought you were satisfied that she'd been there."

"She might not have been there," said Gaunt, " but she might be disinclined to say that she wasn't there. The point is that if she says she was there at that time at least she can prove that someone else in whom she's interested wasn't there."

"I see," said Lanel. "So Geraldine's shielding somebody, is she? And who do you think that is?"

"You," said Gaunt. "And you don't have to argue about it. You've got as much motive for killing Zona as anybody else has. You're keen on Geraldine and you told me that Zona had been making her life a misery."

"Another thing," he went on. "I think it's a bit odd that you should have told Geraldine to go round there and see Zona. I should have thought you might have gone round yourself."

"That would have been clever," said Lanel, "wouldn't it? If I'd gone round there and had a row with Zona I should have lost my job. I should not have been here to keep an eye on Geraldine. I'm not a fool, Gaunt."

"You certainly are not," said Gaunt. "I was very interested in the manner in which you put me on to finding that cupboard behind the bookshelves, the cupboard where Zona used to keep his gun. And the way you concentrated my attention on the carpet. You wouldn't know anything about that suicide set-up I found under Zona's desk, would you? You didn't by any chance arrange it yourself, Lanel?"

Lanel grinned. "All I know about that is what the Detective-Inspector told me," he said.

Gaunt nodded. "That's your story," he said, "but I'm remembering that you had a key to Zona's flat. You were the fellow who was round there and heard the noise of sawing--that was when somebody sawed through those floorboards. You were the fellow who was round there and knew that the books were disarranged and the carpet. It wouldn't take a great deal to make myself or Rickets believe that it was you who did the sawing."

"All right," said Lanel. "You prove it."

"Precisely," said Gaunt. "That's exactly what I said to Ricket when he suggested that I'd put that

                              Peter Cheyney

blank ammunition in Meralda Grey's gun."

He stubbed out his cigarette end in the ashtray on the desk; then he sat back in his chair and took out his cigarette case. He offered a cigarette to Lanel, who took one. Gaunt lit his own cigarette, began to smoke quietly. He was thinking.

Lanel said nothing. He smoked in silence, watching Gaunt.

Eventually Gaunt said: "Well... Ricket's got a few suspects one way and another. At the present moment he's concentrating on Meralda. I suppose he's prepared to take the point of view that I loaded her gun with blank ammunition after she'd killed Gaunt. I should think that would be his case once he can really disprove the suicide theory. I rather imagine that he'll do his best to disprove that theory."

Lanel nodded. He said: "If Ricket can manage to prove that Zona didn't commit suicide, it won't be very good for Meralda. All the circumstantial evidence points to her as being the murderess."

"Does it? That's what you say, and you say it because you want to think it, Lanel."

He leant forward and looked at the secretary, his eyes as hard as steel. "I'm not going to have this job pinned on Meralda," he said quietly. "I rather like Meralda..."

"Who wouldn't?" said Lanel sarcastically.

"Especially now that she's going to be worth about £25,000?"

Gaunt whistled softly. "So that's what Zona left her?" he asked.

Lanel nodded. He was smiling. "It's worth your while to try and prove her innocence, isn't it?" he said. "It would even have been worth while for you to have slipped that blank ammunition into her gun, seeing that Zona's death made her an heiress."

Gaunt blew a smoke ring. He watched it sail across the office. Then he said: "I wouldn't be too keen on trying to hang anything on Meralda if I were you, Lanel. If you do I'm going to make things hot for you."

Lanel raised his eyebrows. "Really," he said cynically, "and how are you going to do that?"

Gaunt said sharply: "If Ricket gets the idea into his head that that suicide set-up was just a fake; if he really decides that Zona didn't commit suicide and begins to look for a murderer, and if he tries to produce a case against Meralda Grey I'm going to let him know that Zona telephoned for Geraldine to hurry round there. I'm going to let him know that she had an appointment with him; I'm going to let him know that you're rather interested in Geraldine; that you advised her to go round there. I'm going to suggest that you might even have gone round there yourself to see what had happened to

Peter Cheyney

her. Have you got any alibi from say six-thirty to seven-thirty?"

Lanel grinned. "Strangely enough I haven't," he said. "I was walking round the West End doing a little quiet thinking."

"I see," said Gaunt. "Well, that lets you in as a possible suspect, too."

Lanel shrugged his shoulders. "I suppose it does," he said.

The detective got up. He began to walk about the office casually. "Of course," he said, "there's just a possibility of another suspect... one we're all forgetting."

Lanel raised his eyebrows. "Not another!" he said. "Who is it this time?"

Gaunt stopped walking. "What about Michael Lorimer?" he asked. "He was supposed to go to Manchester. But we don't know that he went there. He might have got off the train at the first stop and returned to London. There might be a good reason for him doing that. We know he was worried about Meralda. Then he could have another motive. Supposing be knew about Zona's will. Supposing he knew that Zona intended to alter his will, cutting out Meralda Grey. Well... there would be a first-class motive. Lorimer was going to marry Meralda. If she were an heiress he would benefit. If Zona was killed before he had time to alter his will..."

Lanel said nothing. He smoked silently for a while. Then he said: "You cant use that theory. God knows I'm not particularly stuck on Lorimer, he's too goody-goody for me, and he was too inclined to stick his nose into things that didn't concern him, but there's no chance of hanging anything on him.

"I know he went to Manchester. I know that he was going early this morning. He telephoned me at home and told me. He said he was going to try and get a job up there. I told him that if he had any difficulty he'd better go and see Brickett, the manager of the Pirates' Club up there; that Brickett knew a lot of people in Manchester and that he could probably fix Lorimer up.

"Lorimer went to Manchester all right. He telephoned me, from the Pirates' Club after lunch. Brickett wasn't there, but Lorimer had rung him at his house and Brickett had arranged to see Lorimer later in the evening. I was on the telephone to Brickett late tonight. He saw Lorimer and got him a job with a friend of his. So that fixes that. Sorry you can't add Lorimer to the list of suspects."

Gaunt grinned. "That's too bad," he said., "We shall have to eliminate him, so we get back to where we were--the three suspects remain Meralda Grey, Geraldine and you--that is if Zona didn't commit suicide."

He sat down in the chair opposite the desk. He

Peter Cheyney

was smiling. He looked straight at Lanel. "Look here, Lanel," he said, "why don't you and I deal with this thing in the proper way? I'm prepared to play ball if you are."

"Meaning what?" said Lanel. He looked very interested and a little suspicious.

Gaunt lit another cigarette. His face was bland. It wore an open, frank and trusting expression.

He said: "Why should you and I try to make trouble for each other when the solution is so simple. Everything in this case turns on one thing. All we have to do is to deal with that one thing."

"I see," said Lanel. "And what's the one thing?"

"It's just this," said Gaunt coolly. "If Ricket were certain that Meralda Grey's gun was loaded with blank ammunition, that would let her out. Wouldn't it? Once he ceases to suspect her, he would be more inclined to take that suicide theory seriously. Of course if I were to mention to him that Geraldine had been round there and that you were interested in Geraldine, he'd be interested in both of you as possible suspects. But there's no reason why I should mention either of you, providing..."

"Providing what?" asked Lanel.

Gaunt leant across the desk. He looked straight at Lanel. His face was smiling but his eyes were hard.

"Supposing you were able to tell Ricket that

the gun Meralda Grey had was loaded with blank ammunition. Supposing you were able to tell him that at some time or other Lorimer had mentioned to you that the ammunition in the gun was only blank stuff. Possibly I could get Lorimer to support that. He'd say anything to get Meralda out of this situation."

Gaunt paused. Lanel began to smile.

"I'll make a bargain with you," said Gaunt evenly. "You support me on that blank ammunition story and I'm going to forget that Geraldine ever went hear Zone's apartment. Nobody else knows because she went up by the fire-escape. I'll get Lorimer to support the story about the gun being loaded with blanks and Ricket will be able to do nothing at all. He may think a lot but he won't be able to prove anything. He'll probably be glad to fall back on the suicide theory."

"I see," said Lanel. "And Meralda Grey gets the twenty-five thousand under Zona's will and marries that young fool Lorimer. You probably get a nice cut of that money from her for getting her out of this and what do I get?"

"You get this," said Gaunt. "I don't say anything to Ricket about Geraldine or her visit to Zona, or the fact that you're her boy friend and no friend of his. And when I get that cut you mentioned I make it my business to see that you get half. Well...?"

                                    Peter Cheyney

Lanel got up. He was smiling.

"Mr. Gaunt," he said, "it's a deal!"

IX. -- Clever Stuff

GAUNT closed the door of Lanel's office behind him and walked n to the little balcony that ran round the Club floor. He looked at his watch. It was two-thirty. He realised suddenly that he was very tired; he also realised that the very lateness of the hour would prevent Lanel from telephoning through to Geraldine immediately and telling her of his interview with Gaunt and of the deal he had made.

Lanel would not telephone, but would wait until the morning. He would wait because he knew that Geraldine was tired and exhausted.

Gaunt grinned sardonically. This would give him time to do what he wanted to do. Much depended on the interview which he proposed to have with Geraldine before Lanel had a chance to talk to her.

He lit a cigarette and walked towards the club entrance. The place was nearly empty. One or two hardy spirits who had stayed on until the band had obviously begun to yawn were getting their hats and coats at the cloakroom. Gaunt waited until they had gone; then he spoke to the girl behind the counter.

She was the girl to whom he had given the

pound note earlier in the evening.

"Have you got Geraldine's new address?" the detective asked innocently.

"I didn't know she had a new address," the girl replied. "I didn't know she'd moved from Calross street."

Gaunt looked surprised. "I'm getting mixed," he said. "I thought her new address was 15 Calross Street."

The girl shrugged her shoulders. "She may have gone to No. 15 for all I know," she said, "but she was at No. 9 yesterday, because Mr. Lanel sent a note round to her."

Gaunt nodded and went out. Calross Street was quite near the Silver Ring Club. He walked there in a few minutes.

He rang the bell at No. 9 for a good ten minutes before anybody took any notice. Then a bedraggled-looking woman in a red flannel dressing-gown put her head out of the first floor window and asked him what he wanted.

"I am from Scotland Yard," lied Gaunt glibly. "I'm sorry to disturb you at this time, but I've got to have a few words with Miss Nellie Winter."

"All right," said the woman, "I'll tell her."

Two minutes later she opened the door and ushered Gaunt into a dimly-lit hall. On the right was a small sitting-room.

"You wait in there," he said. "I'll send her down to you."

Gaunt lit a cigarette and waited. Five minutes afterwards Geraldine came down. The girl looked tired. There were blue rings beneath her eyes.

She said suspiciously: "You're not a policeman, are you? If you are, why didn't you tell me so when you spoke to me before?"

Gaunt smiled pleasantly. "You sit down and relax, Geraldine," he said. He indicated an armchair on the other side of the dead fire. "Sit down," he repeated, "and smoke a cigarette. I want to have a little talk with you."

He walked over to the door and closed lt. Then he came back and stood looking down at Geraldine.

"You're quite right," he said. 'Tin not a policeman-. You might as well know who I am; My name's Gaunt. I was called in by Mr. Zona last night to investigate some discrepancies in the finances of the club."

He paused for a moment and drew on his cigarette, emitting a cloud of smoke from his nostrils. All the while he was watching Geraldine.

"I've just had a heart-to-heart talk with a friend of yours," he said, "Wolfe Lanel. Both he and I agree that none of us wants a lot of trouble about this Zona killing. I told him that I didn't think there'd be any necessity for him to tell Detective-Inspector

Peter Cheyney

Ricket that you were round at Zona's place tonight."

Her fingers gripped the arms of the chair spasmodically. "How did you know I was round there?" she said. "Did Wolfe tell your?"

"No," said Gaunt airily. "I just happened to find out; and I checked up with him. He knew it would do nobody any good to try and disguise the fact, because somebody saw you"

He sat down in the chair behind him and looked at Geraldine pleasantly.

"The whole point is," he said, "that Miss Grey went round to see Zona tonight and so did you, and somebody else went round there too. Both you and I know who that somebody else was, Geraldine." He shot a sharp look at her. She fell into the trap.

"So Wolfe told you," she said.

Gaunt nodded airily. "What he told me and what I told him is between the two of us," he said. "But the reason that I've come round here at this time in the morning is to fix things up so that we're all going to tell the same sort of story. It wouldn't matter very much about your having gone round to see Zona except for that telephone call that he put through to the Club when he rang through at six-thirty and said you were to hurry." Gaunt paused for a moment and took a chance. "Why didn't you go round there right away?" he said.

"How could I?" said Geraldine. "When I had a

talk with Wolfe earlier in the afternoon about it, he said I ought to go round and see Zona. He said he'd come round with me. While we were talking Zona came through to the office and asked to speak to me. He said I was to come round about six-fifteen. He said he'd have the double windows in the bedroom open so that I could get in by the fire-escape.

"But I didn't want to go. I didn't want to go round there on my own. I've had plenty of trouble from Zona before. I expect Wolfe's told you he's not a particularly nice sort of man, especially when he's keen on a girl."

Gaunt nodded. "And he was keen on you?" he said.

She smiled. "Too keen for my liking."

Gaunt said easily: "If Zona was making life troublesome for you, Geraldine, why didn't you pack up and get out? A nice-looking girl like you can easily get herself another job."

"That's what I said," she answered. "But I stayed on because of Wolfe. Wolfe wanted me to stay on."

The detective nodded. "All right," he said. "Go on with the story."

"Wolfe said the thing for me to do would be to wait until he could come round with me; that we'd both go round together; that he'd talk to Zona. Then some business turned up and he couldn't go. He said the best thing I could do would be to go

                                    Peter Cheyney

round on my own, but to get there late, so that he'd have time to get through his business and get round there just about the same time, or immediately after I got there."

"I see." said Gaunt "So then you went off somewhere? You left the club before six-thirty--before Zona telephoned through for you."

"Yes," she said, "I came home here. I changed my frock and hung about for a bit. I didn't want to see Zona on my own. I started to go round there just after seven o'clock, and when I got into the alleyway at the back of the Colindale Apartments, I saw Wolfe coming down the steps of the fire-escape. I called out to him but he didn't hear me. He was almost at the bottom and turned and went out the other way. I wondered why he hadn't waited, and then I thought it was probably because he thought I might be coming from the other side of the Square; that he was going to wait for me at the other end of the passage.

"I thought I was right about this, because when I was half way up the fire-escape I looked over the side, end he turned and began walking back, he looked up and saw me and I waved my hand to him. I continued up the fire-escape. When I got to the top the double windows were unlocked. I turned round and saw that Wolfe had begun to come up after me, so I pushed open the windows and stepped into Zona's bedroom.

"The door between his bedroom and his study was half-way open. Through it I could see the right-hand side of the study. I could see Zona's right arm and a bit of his shoulder. His hand was on his desk and there was a pistol in it---a pistol with a string tied to one end of it.

"I felt awful. Wolfe had told me once or twice that he wouldn't be surprised if Zona committed suicide one day. I thought that was what he'd done. All I wanted to do was to get out. I stepped through the windows, closed them behind me and started to walk down the fire-escape steps towards Wolfe.

"I asked him What was the matter with Zona. I asked him why he hadn't stopped when I came into the passage; that I'd seen him coming down the fire-escape. He asked me what the devil I meant, and I told him that through the door I had seen Zona's arm on the desk with a pistol in his hand; that by the position of his arm and hand it looked as if he was dead

"Wolfe said: 'My God, let's get out of this.' We looked into the passage below. There was no one there. We walked through into the Square and be-gan to walk towards Mount Street. Wolfe told me that he'd arrived earlier; that when he'd gone into the passage behind the Colindale Apartments he'd thought I might have gone up to Zona's flat; that

Peter Cheyney

he'd gone up the fire-escape, opened the windows and looked into Zona's study, but there was no one there.

"He said the door leading from the study into the hallway was closed; that he'd thought Zona must be out, and that as I was late he had come down again to meet me. He said that Zona must have been in the hallway when he looked into the room; that during the time he'd been coming down the fire-escape and walking along the passage thinking it would enter it from the other end, and my going up and looking into the room, Zona must have come back, taken up the pistol and killed himself.

"Wolfe asked me how I knew that Zona was dead if I hadn't gone into the study. I said that I didn't know; but that it looked like it."

Gaunt said nothing. He sat in the chair drawing on his cigarette. He didn't believe the story that Geraldine had told him, although he realised that she might think she was telling the truth.

The detective, whose mind went straight to essential points, realised that it was unlikely, if Zona was going out, that he would have left the double windows unlocked.

Gaunt thought that Zona had not gone out but that possibly it suited Lanel to tell that story to Geraldine; he had to tell her something.

He got up. "Thanks, Geraldine," he said. "Of

course I knew all this. Lanel told me most of it. Anyhow, the whole thing's very simple. We just forget about your visit to Zona's flat, that's all."

Geraldine nodded. She looked a little less unhappy. "I don't care who says what so long as I am kept out of this," she said. "I don't like it. I was frightened of Zona when he was alive, and now he's dead I'm even more frightened."

Gaunt picked up his hat. "I shouldn't worry if I were you," he said. "There's only take person who's got to worry on this job."

She looked at him quickly. "Who's that?" she asked.

Gaunt grinned. "The person who killed Zona," he said. "Goodnight Geraldine." He went out.

Gaunt walked slowly back to his flat near his Conduit Street office.

He realised he was tired. When things happened they happened all at once. He let his mind wander back during the last four hours, realised that he had hardly stopped moving or thinking since that afternoon. He wondered what the next day would bring forth.

IT was ten o'clock when Gaunt woke. While he was bathing and dressing he was turning over in his mind the interview which he intended to have with Ricket. He thought it might be a rather odd sort of

 Peter Cheyney

interview. He also thought he would not go round to Scotland Yard yet awhile. He wanted to give Lanel lots of time to see Geraldine; to discover how he had been tricked by the detective into telling him the story of what had happened to them both when they had gone to Zona's flat. Lanel would be furious; he would regret the deal he had made. He might do anything. Gaunt grinned at the thought.

It was eleven o'clock when he got to his office. Josephine Dark brought in his correspondence and Gaunt began to read his letters. He was barely half way through the first one when the telephone jangled. He took off the receiver, it was Meralda Grey.

"Mr. Gaunt," she said, "I thought I'd better tell you that the police are here. There is a Detective-Sergeant from Scotland Yard in the next room. He's been sent round here by Detective-Inspector Ricket. He says I'm to go with him to the Yard. They want me to make a statement."

Gaunt smiled into the telephone. "That's all right, Meralda," he said, "and I hope you don't mind me calling you Meralda, because I always think of you that way. Don't worry. Go round to Scotland Yard and tell Detective-Inspector Ricket anything that he wants to know, and I shouldn't take him too seriously either. He can ask as many questions as he likes, but he can't disprove the fact that the ammunition in the pistol you had was only blank. Keep your chin up; I'll give you a ring some time this afternoon."

"I must say you're very comforting," she said. "I hope it's going to be like you say. Goodbye, Mr. Gaunt."

"Just a minute," said Gaunt. "You haven't by any chance telephoned anybody else, have you, while that Detective-Sergeant was waiting round there?"

"Yes, I have," she said. "I telephoned Michael in Manchester and told him. I had a letter from him this morning."

"I see," said Gaunt "And what did he say?"

"Just the same as you did;" she replied. "He told me not to worry. He said he was returning to town immediately; that when he got to town he'd go straight to Scotland Yard and give them the surprise, of their lives."

"You don't say," said Gaunt. He was smiling. "Well, that will be nice for them, won't it? Well, don't worry. I'll ring you this afternoon. Goodbye, Meralda."

He hung up. After he had put the receiver back on its hook he sat there for a few moments looking at it. His grin was more sardonic than ever. Things were working out the way he thought they would.

X. -- The Confession

IT was twelve-thirty when Gaunt got up from his desk, put on his hat, and strolled into the outer office. He said to Josephine Dark: "I'm going out to lunch. If Ricket rings through and wants to speak to me, tell him you don't know where I am. Say you expect me back some time this afternoon."

While he was eating his lunch Gaunt permitted his mind to wander over the rather extraordinary story that Geraldine had told him of the visit paid by her and Wolfe Lanel to Zona's flat

He found it difficult to understand Wolfe Lanel's remark on hearing from Geraldine that she believed that Zona was dead. Lanel had said: "Let's get out of this..." Hardly the sort of remark made by an innocent man who had just been told that his employer had committed suicide.

His excuse that they did not want to be mixed up with the business was flimsy. Gaunt believed that it would have been natural for Lanel to have immediately inspected the body--even out of curiosity--and then telephoned the police. Why had he not done so?

It was three o'clock when he returned to the office. He went into his room and telephoned through to Scotland Yard at once. He asked for

Ricket. When the Detective-Inspector came on the line Gaunt said:

"Hello, Ricket. I am ringing you up to find out how things are going There are one or two things I'd like to talk over with you."

"You don't say so," Ricket replied. His voice was rather grim "There are one or two things I want to talk over with you, too. I think you're going to find yourself in a bit of a jam before you're very much older."

"Oh, yes," said Gaunt, "and what am I supposed to do--burst into tears? What's the trouble. Ricket?'

Ricket said: "I sent a detective-sergeant round to Meralda Grey's place this morning. I thought it was time we had an official statement from that young woman. I said he was to bring her round here; that I wanted to talk to her. She said that was all right; that she'd come, but that she'd like to do some telephoning first. She went into the bedroom and closed the door. What she didn't know was that I have had her telephone tapped since yesterday evening. I've got a précis of her conversations in front of me at the moment.

"Her first call was to Manchester She spoke to her boy friend, Michael Lorimer. She told him about Zona's murder, and said she was suspected of committing it; that a policeman was waiting to take her to the Yard. He said she was not to worry; that

                     Peter Cheyney

he knew she must be innocent; that he was coming up to town right away, and that when he got up here he'd give us a big surprise. That was her first telephone call.

"The second one was to you at your office, so you know all about that one."

There was a pause, then Gaunt said: "Yes, I would know all about that one, wouldn't I?" He was still grinning.

"We'll come back to that second conversation in a minute," the Detective-Inspector continued. "About twenty minutes later this fellow Michael Lorimer rang me up from Manchester. He was at the railway station waiting for his train. He told me that I needn't bother to take a statement from Meralda Grey, because he was the person who had killed Zona.

"I said that was very interesting I asked him at what time he killed Zona and how he got into the flat. He said he'd shot him at five o'clock in the afternoon, and that he'd got into the flat by the fire-escape stairs and through the double windows, which were open."

Gaunt laughed. "Well, that's a nice confession anyway," he said

"Confession my eye," said Ricket 'It's rubbish! First of all we know that fellow was in Manchester yesterday. He couldn't have been in town at five o'clock. Secondly, we know that Zona was alive and well after six, because he telephoned down to the hall porter at the Colindale Apartments and gave him some instructions. We've checked on the time that call was made. It was six fifty-five. So we know that Zona was alive then,"

"And the hall-porter was certain that it was Zona speaking?" asked Gaunt.

"He's dead certain of it," said Ricket.

"I see," said Gaunt. "That's very interesting, isn't it, Ricket? And so you believe that this confession is nonsense?"

"It's unutterable rubbish," said Ricket, "and you know it. Another thing, you know why he's making it too."

"Do I?" queried Gaunt innocently. "Well, why is he making it?"

"He's making it because he knows that Meralda Grey killed Zona. Because he knows that she killed him with a pistol he gave her before he went to Manchester. He realised he was a fool to have given her that pistol; he probably didn't think she'd use it at the time. Now he's doing his best to get her out of this jam. Anyway, he'll be here at four o'clock. I shall be able to talk to him."

Gaunt said: "You seem pretty certain in your mind, Ricket, that Meralda Grey killed Zona."

"I am," said Ricket. "I'm more than certain

now." Gaunt noticed the stress on the last word.

"Why, Ricket?" he asked. "What have you learnt recently that has confirmed your original suspicion?"

There was a moment's silence. Then Ricket said, "Listen, Rufus, you and I have always been more or less friendly in an odd sort of way, but I want to warn you to watch your step. When I tell you why I'm certain that the Grey woman killed Zona now you'll understand why you've to watch your step. Do you know a fellow called Wolfe Lanel?"

"I do," said Gaunt. "A very nice fellow--Zona's secretary."

"All right," said Ricket. "Well, Lanel's been round here this morning. Lanel tells me that you admitted to him last night that you loaded Meralda Grey's gun with that blank ammunition after Zona had been shot, so now your theory that she couldn't have killed Zona because there were no real bullets in the gun is washed out once and for all. So far as I am concerned any suicide angle in this Zona killing is right out."

Gaunt made a clicking noise with his tongue. His face was quite placid.

"Things are beginning to look pretty bad for me, aren't they, Ricket?" he asked. "In a minute you'll be telling me that I'm an accessory to Zona's murder; that I went round there and held Meralda Grey's hand while she did it."

Ricket said: "Well, Gaunt, we shall want an explanation from you, and it had better be a good one."

"It will be," said Gaunt. "My explanations always are. By the way, you say you expect Lorimer at four o'clock. Don't you think it would be a good thing for me to come down then? And where's Meralda Grey? what have you done with her?"

"I've let her go home," said the police officer. "But she's under observation. I couldn't very well hold her until I'd satisfied myself that Lorimer was talking rubbish. I've taken a statement from her. She told me what happened. She said that she never looked at the ammunition in that gun and doesn't know whether it was blank or ball ammunition, She says you told her it was blank on the telephone after the murder, and she believes it for a very good reason. She wanted to believe it."

"All very nice," said Gaunt, "well, I'll be down at four o'clock, Ricket."

"Very Well," said Ricket.

Gaunt hung up. He looked quite happy.

IT was half-past four. Ricket, sitting behind his desk in his room at Scotland Yard, regarded Michael Lorimer and Gaunt with a cynical smile.

Gaunt, a cigarette hanging from his lips, was

                                Peter Cheyney

watching Lorimer. The young man looked a picture of utter depression. His hands gripped the arms of his chair spasmodically and he looked from Ricket to Gaunt and back again miserably.

"It's no good, Mr. Lorimer," said Ricket. "I can understand how you feel. I can even sympathise with you. At the same time you've got to understand that the police are not here to be made fools of. This so-called confession of yours is rubbish. Whichever way you look at it, it won't stand the most superficial examination.

"You say that you killed Zona at some time about five o'clock. We know that he was alive after six; that at six fifty-five he telephoned down to the hall-porter and gave him some instructions. When I asked you where Zona was when you shot him you told me that he was standing in front of his desk. That is quite impossible. He was sitting behind his desk. When I asked you which side of the head you fired at you said the left side. Well, the bullet that killed Zona entered his head from the right-hand side."

Ricket took a cigarette from the box on his desk and lit it. He looked at Lorimer and smiled.

"Taking all things into consideration, for a man who says that he's committed a murder, you don't seem to know very much about it," the Detective-Inspector went on. "And finally and perhaps most importantly of all, there's the fact that we knew that you were somewhere else at the time you tell us you killed Zona. You were in Manchester. You were there at the Pirates Club soon after lunch trying to find where the manager was--the man who was going to get you a job. The only way you could have got up to London by five o'clock would have been by airplane and you didn't do that. We've checked up and know you didn't."

Ricket got up. He came round the desk and put his hand on Lorimer's shoulder.

"It's tough luck " he said. "And I don't know that I don't admire you for trying to shoulder the blame. We know who killed Zona... and it wasn't you. You get back to your work in Manchester and forget all about this... and Meralda Grey. I don't think she's the sort of girl friend for a decent fellow like you "

Lorimer got up. Gaunt got up, too. They walked to the door together.

"By the way, Gaunt," said Ricket as they were about to leave the room, "I'm going to do you a good turn and forget about that nonsense you told me about that pistol being loaded with blanks I'd advise you to forget about it too." He smiled cynically. "I'd give this case up if I were you, Gaunt, and not waste any more of your time--or mine--with faked evidence."

Gaunt grinned. "Thanks, Ricket," he said

Peter Cheyney

amiably. "Maybe I'll take your advice and maybe not. Good-day."

He closed the door behind him.

Outside in the corridor he took Michael Lorimer by the arm.

'It's tough luck," he said. "I knew that Ricket was wise to you directly he told me that you'd told him on the telephone that you'd shot Zona at five o'clock. I realised at once that he'd know that was rubbish because of the hall-porter's evidence. If Zona hadn't telephoned to the hall-porter at six-fifty-five you might have got away with it and got yourself charged with murder." He grinned happily. "That is, if Ricket hadn't happened to know that you were in Manchester on the day of the murder. Anyhow, let's go somewhere and get a cup of tea. I want to talk to you."

Lorimer said: "This is all too awful. I just can't believe it. I can't believe that Meralda did it. I won't believe it."

Gaunt shrugged his shoulders. "I'm afraid you'll have to get yourself in the frame of mind in which you can face the fact that Ricket will charge Meralda with murder within the next twenty-four hours," he said grimly, "Because that's what he's going to do."

Lorimer nodded miserably. As they crossed the road and walked towards Victoria Street he stumbled and nearly fell. The detective caught him by the arm.

"Take it easy," he said. "And don't lose your nerve. You'll do no good by panicking. With a bit of luck we'll find a way out for Meralda yet."

"Do you think there's a chance of it... even a mere hope?" asked Lorimer.

Gaunt nodded. "I do," he said. "There is just a chance. As a matter of fact, if it hadn't been for Lanel I might have got away with my original scheme. I expect Ricket told you about the information I have given him that the gun Meralda had with her was loaded with blanks. The whole success of that little scheme depended upon the time that I discovered that fact. Unfortunately, I told Lanel that I was the fellow who had slipped the blank ammunition into the gun. He promptly gave the information to Ricket, and that was the end of that. I'd hoped to get at you before Ricket had a chance to talk to you and get you to support my story, to say that you had loaded the pistol with blank ammunition before you gave it to Meralda. But Ricket got in first, so that's that."

They went into a tea-shop in Victoria Street. Gaunt could see that Lorimer was on the verge of a breakdown. His hand was trembling as he carried his tea-cup to his lips.

After a while Lorimer said: "I think you're being

pretty decent about all this business, Gaunt. Ricket told me that you were engaged by Zona to look after his interests. I suppose Zona told you a lot of fairy stories about me?"

Gaunt nodded. "Yes," he said. "But I didn't have to believe them." He grinned. "I've always had my own ideas about the sort of person Mario Zona was," he added.

Lorimer attempted a smile. "Anyhow," he said, "I don't know what your reasons are, but you've certainly done your best far Meralda. You've done everything you could to get her out of this horrible mess."

"We both have," said the detective. "And," he added, his eyes twinkling, "We've net finished yet."

He leant across the table. "I've still got a trump card up my sleeve. I'm just biding my time to play it."

Lorimer opened his eyes wide. "You've really got something?" he queried. "You're not just trying another fake on Ricket?"

"Not this time," said Gaunt. "But whatever happens I've got to have your support. Where are you staying?"

"I shall be at the Vine Hotel in Aldwych," Lorimer answered.

"All right," said Gaunt. "Now you go there and stay there. Don't try and see Meralda. Just go to your hotel and relax. I'm going to get into touch with you tonight. I'll telephone you some time after eight o'clock. I'll probably ask you to meet me somewhere where we can talk. I've got an idea--a very definite idea--but I'm not quite certain about it yet."

"I'll do anything," said Lorimer. "Anything possible, to help. But can't I know something about this scheme of yours?"

"Not at the moment," said Gaunt "I said it was a trump card, and I'm going to keep it up my sleeve until the time comes to play it. When the time arrives I promise you'll be there."

XI. -- The Thin End of the Wedge

GAUNT stood for a moment in Victoria Street watching the figure of Michael Lorimer disappear in the dusk. Then he began to walk towards Whitehall. Half-way down he stopped a passing cab and told the driver to take him to Colindale Apartments. Just inside the entrance he found the hall-porter. Gaunt handed the man a ten shilling note.

"My name's Gaunt," he said. "I'm a private detective. I was doing some work for Mr. Zona when he was killed. Perhaps you could give me a little information."

"Anything I can, sir," said the hall-porter. "What is it you want to know?"

Gaunt lit a cigarette. "I was at Scotland Yard this afternoon," he said. "Detective-Inspector Ricket said that you told him that Mr. Zona telephoned down to you from his apartment at six fifty-five yesterday."

"That's right," said the man.

"Are you sure that was the exact time," asked the detective.

"Absolutely certain, sir," said the hall-porter.

There's a clock in the hall here. I can see it from the office. It's an electric clock and its always dead right. I go off at seven o'clock and I looked at that clock as Mr. Zona telephoned down."

Gaunt nodded. "I see," he said. "That settles that it was six fifty-five. Now what was it Mr. Zona said to you?"

"He asked me to go round to the chemist and get a bottle of spirits of alcohol. I said all right, although I was a bit annoyed because I had a date and I was in a hurry to get away. I just got to the doorway when the telephone rang again. "

"I went back and answered it. It was Mr. Zona, again. He said I needn't bother; and he didn't want the spirits of alcohol."

"And you're sure it was Zona?" said Gaunt.

"Absolutely," said the man. "I'd swear to it. I'd know his voice in a million, sir."

"Thanks," said Gaunt. He went out.

Outside, he picked up a passing cab and drove to Meralda Grey's flat. As he rang the bell he noticed a man--obviously a plainclothes man--standing on the other side of the road. Gaunt grinned. Ricket was taking no chances about Meralda trying to make a getaway.

When the maid showed him into her sitting-room she was standing in front of the fire, her hands on the mantelpiece, looking down into the flames. Her eyes were rimmed with dark circles. She looked terribly ill. She turned as he came into the room. He smiled at her cheerfully.

"You know, Meralda," he said, "I think you're taking all this business a trifle too seriously. Sit down and relax."

He offered her his cigarette case, produced a lighter, lit a cigarette for her.

"It is rather difficult to feel otherwise," she said. "And I wonder how you can expect me to feel cheerful, Mr. Gaunt. I suppose I've been deluding myself all along. Now I'm faced with stark reality. I am a murderess. I killed Zona."

Gaunt nodded. "Exactly," he said. That's what you think, but I don't."

She looked at him sharply. "You don't really mean that," she said. "You're just trying to give me some sort of hope."

"No, I'm not," said Gaunt. "I'm talking hard sense, but I've got to be certain this time, and I've got to be able to prove what I think. Ricket will be very suspicious now that Lanel has told him that I put that blank ammunition in that automatic pistol after Zona had been shot." He grinned again. "Which is exactly what I thought he'd do," he concluded.

She looked at him in surprise. "So you meant him to tell Detective-Inspector Ricket that?" he asked.

Gaunt nodded. "Yes," he said. "I knew that once Ricket believed that my evidence about the blank ammunition in that pistol was fake, he'd send a police officer round here to pick you up. I wanted you picked up. You see, I thought the time had come for this job to be brought to a head."

She looked, at him in amazement. '

"Mr Gaunt," she said, her cigarette hanging limply in her fingers, "are you trying to tell me that I didn't kill Zona?"

"Definitely," said Gaunt. "I'll go even farther. I know it is quite impossible for you to have killed Zona."

Her blue eyes were big with astonishment. "Why do you say that?" she asked.

Gaunt said: "I want to ask questions, not answer them. Now listen carefully. Yesterday evening you telephoned through to my office and told me that you had shot Zona. That was at ten past seven. How long was it since you'd left Zona's flat?"

She thought for a moment. "My telephone call to you would be within fifteen minutes of my leaving there," she said.

Gaunt nodded. "That's what I thought," he said cheerfully. "Now I want you to promise not to go out of this flat, not to telephone anybody, not to see anybody until I give you permission. Are you going to be good?"

She smiled pathetically. "I can't be anything else," she said. I have got to trust somebody, and strangely enough--and I don't know the reason--I'm inclined to trust you, Mr. Gaunt."

Gaunt grinned. "That's fine," he said. "Now answer one more question. Did you know that Zona had left you most of his money?"

She paused for a moment. Then she said: "He'd hinted once of twice that he was leaving me some money. He said that he was going to look after his old friend's daughter, or some such remark. I have worried about it very much."

Gaunt said: "Would you be surprised to hear that Zona had left you £25,000?"

"Yes, I would," she said.

"Well, that's what he's done," said Gaunt. "Lanel told me about the will. There's just one other thing before I go. I shall probably ring tonight, and I'll ask you a question. I shall want you to tell me if you receive any telephone messages here and what they are. Will you do that?"

"I'll do anything you , say," she said. "I've told you that I trust you."

"Good girl," said Gaunt. "Now don't worry. I'll ring you some time tonight. Au revoir."

He closed the door behind him.

OUTSIDE in the street Gaunt looked at

his watch. It was six thirty. He stood for a moment, lighting a cigarette, working out his plan of campaign. Then he hailed a cab and drove to The Silver Ring Club.

The place was almost deserted. The girl in the cloakroom was dusting the empty shelves and one or two tired-looking waiters were sweeping the dance-floor and arranging tables for dinner.

Gaunt walked round the balcony, through the pass-door and stood silently in front of the office door. Then, without knocking, he opened it and stepped into the room.

Lanel was sitting in his usual position behind the desk. Pacing him, smoking a cigarette, was Geraldine.

"Good evening," said Gaunt cheerfully.

He took out his cigarette case, selected a cigarette. Lanel watched him coolly.

"I wanted to have a word with you, Lanel," said Gaunt. "And it's just as well that Geraldine's here."

Lanel shrugged his shoulders. "There's nothing you can say to me that anybody couldn't hear," he said. "Although I should have imagined that you'd have had enough of this case by this time. I can imagine that Ricket isn't too pleased with you."

Gaunt grinned. "Don't be a fool, Lanel," he said. "I suppose you think that because you informed him that I'd told you that I slipped that blank

                                    Peter Cheyney

ammunition into Meralda Grey's gun after Zona was killed, I'd get frightened."

He pulled up a chair and sat down.

"I made a deal with you," said Lanel. "The bargain was that you weren't going to say anything about Geraldine's having gone round to Zona's flat. I, on my part, was going to support you in the story that Lorimer had told me some time ago that his automatic--the one he gave Meralda Grey--was loaded only with blank ammunition. Well, I consider you walked out on that deal. You went straight away from this office and bluffed Geraldine into telling you what happened when she and I went round to Zona's place. That made me distrust you. So I told Ricket that your story about the blank ammunition was false.

Gaunt nodded cheerfully. "But you didn't tell him about your Geraldine's visit to Zona's flat. You didn't think that mattered, I suppose?"

"No, I didn't," said Lane! "And neither does it. Geraldine here can support anything I have to say about that visit."

Gaunt grinned. "Can she?" he asked sardonically. "Or do you mean that Geraldine can support what you told her. Geraldine's evidence is useless. She saw you coming down the fire-escape from Zona's flat when she entered the passage. She saw you turn and go down the passage towards the

Berkeley Square end, but she's only got your word for what you saw in Zona's flat when you were up there, and she's only got your word for what you did."

Lanel stiffened. "What do you mean by that?" he asked.

"I mean that what you told Geraldine was just a packet of damned lies," said Gaunt, still grinning. "I know what you saw when you went up that fire-escape before Geraldine arrived. You didn't see her when you were coming down, otherwise you'd have stopped her. As it was you hurried towards the Berkeley Square end of the passage, hoping to meet her and stop her. When you came back you saw her on the fire-escape. You dashed up and met her on her way down. When she told you what she had seen you said: 'My God, let's get out Of this!' Well... why did you say that? If you were ignorant of what had happened in the flat why didn't you go up and look for yourself? Why didn't you telephone the police?".

"Why should I?" said Lanel. "What had it go to do with me? I didn't want either of us to get mixed up in a scandal."

"And you expect me to believe that?" asked Gaunt. "Why, I can see by the look on Geraldine's face at this moment that she thinks I'm right. And there's another thing, Lanel. Geraldine had an appointment to see Zona earlier that afternoon. She came to you and told you about it. She told you that she didn't want to go round to Zona's place because she was afraid of him. I believe that to be true. Well, what did you do? You told her to keep the appointment, but that you would go with her. But you didn't go with her. You kept her hanging about while you did some business or other; you made her so late for her original appointment that Zona had to telephone through here and tell her to hurry--that was at six-thirty--and then what did you do? After being so keen on her not going round by herself, you deliberately sent her round by herself saying that you would go round and meet her. When you got there she hadn't arrived. You went up to the flat and saw something that surprised you. You came dashing down and ran to the Berkeley Square end of the passage to stop her, but you were too late. She'd come by the other end of the passage.

"But even then it was all right because she'd only seen Zona's arm and shoulder. She'd only seen his hand holding the pistol with the string attached to it. She believed that he'd committed suicide. If you'd telephoned the police and told them they'd have wanted to know what you were doing round there. They'd have wanted to ask all sorts of inconvenient questions, wouldn't they, Lanel? So you said: 'My

God, let's get out of this,' and hoped that no one had seen either of you going up the fire-escape. And you were lucky. Nobody did."

Lanel lit a cigarette. His air of nonchalance had departed. Gaunt could see that the hand that held the cigarette lighter was not very steady.

"Well... if nobody saw us. that's that," said Lanel. "There's only your word that Geraldine told you what had happened., And our word's as good as yours."

Gaunt laughed. "That's true enough, Lanel," he said. "But you've forgotten something else. You've forgotten your telephone call to Manchester yesterday at mid-day. Why did you telephone through to Manchester to speak to Michael Lorimer? How did you know that he was in Manchester? Meralda Grey only persuaded him to go there early yesterday morning. She saw him off in the train. Yet you knew he was there. You telephoned through to the Pirates Club and you spoke to Lorimer."

Gaunt stopped speaking and looked at Lanel sharply. He saw that there were little beads of sweat on the secretary's forehead. He looked at Geraldine. She was looking at Lanel. Her eyes were wide with astonishment.

Gaunt began to grin again.

"You're surprised, aren't you. Geraldine?" he said. "Even you are beginning to wonder just what your boy friend here has been playing at."

He stubbed out his cigarette, lit another. "Perhaps you'd like me to tell you why you telephoned through to Manchester. All right, I will."

He leaned back in his chair. His voice was level.

"When you realised that Zona had called me in the night before last to do a little investigating, you weren't so happy," he said. "Possibly you had good reason for that. Maybe you were responsible for some of the defalcations that Zona was worrying about. Anyhow, you got into Zona's office here early the next morning and you had a look through his private papers. You found what you wanted to find. You found that will. Something happened during the morning that made it necessary for you to telephone to Manchester, didn't it, Lanel? And I know what that something was, You see, I'm a good guesser!"

Lanel said nothing. His eyes were frightened.

Gaunt said: "You watch your step. Things aren't going to be too good for you as it is, but if you try any more funny business, if you get in my way again, you're going to be for it. I'm going to see that you're charged as being accessory to murder and that means that Geraldine will be charged as being accessory, too. Do you understand that?"

Gaunt got up. He stood looking down at Lanel.

"You take a tip from me, Lanel." he said. "The

best thing for you to do is to keep yourself out of even more trouble. My advice to you is to stay here and keep Geraldine here. I've an idea that Ricket will he sending someone round here to talk to you tonight. If he does, remember that there's nothing like the truth. Well, so long, Lanel. Au revoir, Geraldine!"

He flipped his hat over one eye and went out. When he had gone Lanel looked at Geraldine. His fact was grim.

She said: "So you've been kidding me, Wolfe. You'd better tell me the truth."

XII. -- The Letter

IT was nine o'clock.

Gaunt, sitting at his desk in his office, could hear the patter of the rain on the windows. He stubbed out his cigarette with an air of decision. Then he took off the telephone receiver and rang Ricket at Scotland Yard.

He said: "I think it's about time that you and I put our cards down on the table, Ricket."

Ricket said: "That'll be a nice change as far as you're concerned Gaunt. But I don't know that I'm interested in your cards."

"All right," said Gaunt. "Well, perhaps you'll tell me something. I suppose you're thinking about arresting Meralda Grey?"

"I am," said Ricket. "The Commissioner has all the papers and information before him now. I'm waiting for an instruction from him to arrest her on the murder charge at any moment."

"I see," said Gaunt. "Well, let me give you a tip. I'd hate to see you make a fool of yourself, Ricket, but I can promise you this much. If you do arrest Meralda Grey, you'll be a laughing stock."

"I see," said Ricket caustically. "Have you got some more funny evidence to produce like that stuff about the blank ammunition?"

Gaunt said: "Just listen to this, and listen hard. I told Lanel that I slipped that blank ammunition into Meralda Grey's gun after Zona was killed. Well, that wasn't true. It might interest you to know that I loaded her gun with blank ammunition in my office before she went round to Zona's flat. Not only did I do it then, but I did it in the presence of my secretary, Josephine Dark, in the outside office. I've got the original clip of ball cartridges that I took out of that gun here in my office drawer. And how do you like that?"

There was a pause. From the other end of the wire came an exclamation.

"I thought that would surprise you," said Gaunt. "Now listen Ricket. I take it that you want to arrest somebody for killing Zona. You and I both know he didn't commit suicide. I know that Meralda Grey didn't kill him. I know who did. If you want to arrest the murderer you can do it tonight. But you'll have to do it in my way,"

Ricket said, "What an annoying cuss you are, Gaunt. What have you got up your sleeve?"

"Plenty," the detective answered. "Now here's what I want you to do. First of all I suggest that you send somebody round to the Silver Ring Club and pick up Wolfe Lanel and Geraldine. I saw Lanel not long ago. I had a very straight talk with that gentleman, and I left him in a state of mind in which he'll

                    Peter Cheyney

probably be only too glad to make things easy for himself by telling the truth.

"I suggest that you fill in the time by taking a statement from him and Geraldine. If you take the statements separately, you'll find they'll fit in with each other. Then there's something else I want you to do, but I'd rather not talk about it on the telephone. I'll come round and see you."

"All right," said Ricket, "I'll be here. But I hope you can prove what you're saying Gaunt."

Gaunt grinned. "Don't worry, Ricket," he said. "I've got my own methods of working. I'll be with you in a quarter of an hour. Just possess your soul in patience."

He hung up and leant back in his chair, lit another cigarette and amused himself for a few minutes by blowing smoke rings. Then he got up, went into the outer office, found a telephone directory and looked up the number of the Vine Hotel in Aldwych. He went back to his desk, rang through to the hotel and asked for Mr. Lorimer. He was put through at once. Lorimer's voice, tense and expectant, came over the line:

"Is that you, Gaunt? Have you been successful?"

"I don't know," said Gaunt. "But something's happened that can change the whole complexion of this case, something that may easily prove that Meralda is innocent."

"That's wonderful," said Lorimer, "What has happened?"

"It appears," said Gaunt, "that yesterday evening, some time after six o'clock, Zona wrote a letter. This letter was addressed to me. He sent it down to the hall porter and told him to take it straight round to my office. Now its certain that that letter was important--very important--because Zona knew that I was going to see him at seven-thirty.

"The hall-porter says," Gaunt continued, lying glibly, "that Zona had had a telephone call just before he wrote that letter."

"I see," said Lorimer. "What was in the letter?"

"I don't know," said Gaunt, "because the idiot never delivered it. He put it to his pocket and then some other business turned up and he forgot it. He's off duty now. and he found the letter about an hour ago. He's just telephoned through here saying that he'll bring it round to my office tonight before he goes on duty at ten o'clock."

Gaunt put a note of tense excitement into his voice.

"Supposing for the sake of argument," he said, "that the telephone call Zona received just before he wrote that letter was from the murderer. Supposing Zona knew that he was in danger and sent off a note to me immediately, telling me to come round, telling me the name of the person who'd telephoned him."

Lorimer said: "Have you any idea--any inkling who it would be?"

"Yes," said Gaunt, "I think the person mentioned in that note was Wolfe Lanel."

Lorimer said: "What do you want me to do?"

"Nothing very much," said Gaunt. "But I thought you'd be interested to know what was in that letter. The hall-porter says he'll have it round here about ten o'clock. I suggest you come round at ten-fifteen. There'll be nobody here except myself. Don't come through the outer office; walk along the corridor and tap on the door of my private office. I'll leave the street door open for you."

"Right," said Lorimer. "I'll be with you at ten-fifteen."

Gaunt hung up. He was grinning. Then he got up, put on his hat and overcoat, and took a cab to Scotland Yard.

RICKET looked at Gaunt over his desk. He looked worried.

He said: "I hope you're not making any mistakes this time, Rufus. I hope this new theory of yours is going to pan out."

Gaunt shrugged his shoulders.

"I've told you," he said, "that I loaded the blank ammunition into Meralda Grey's gun before she went round to see Zona. That means she didn't kill him, and that in turn means somebody else did. You're going to know who that somebody else is tonight."

Ricket nodded gloomily.

"Well, I hope you're right," he said. "The Commissioner considers that there's a cut-and-dried case against Meralda Grey. He believes that we can't fail to secure a conviction on our evidence."

He looked at Gaunt sharply.

"You haven't got anything on that fellow Lanel, by any chance?" he said. "Or Geraldine. I've discovered that there was something between Zona and Geraldine. Have you?"

Gaunt said: "You're not going to make me talk before I want to. Now, first of all I'd like to put a few points up to you, Ricket--odd points which I consider to be definite pointers towards the murderer I want you to remember them. They'll be useful to you a little later tonight.

"First of all let's go back to yesterday afternoon. Let's go back to the time that Meralda Grey came into my office. When she came to see me she made no attempt to conceal the fact that she had the automatic pistol in her handbag. That struck me as hardly being the point of view of a potential murderess--of a woman who was on her way to use that pistol. But some instinct prompted me not to take

Peter Cheyney

any chances.

"I knew that Meralda Grey was a hot-tempered young woman. I told her that I had a pistol of the same make, but with a slight difference in the safety catch. And I walked into the outer office to get my own pistol, taking hers with me. I knew that I had a clip of blank ammunition in the drawer. I took it out, loaded it into her automatic in place of the clip of ball cartridges, which I handed to Josephine Dark, my secretary. That clip is in the office now.

"It is lucky for Meralda Grey that I did do that, because she did lose her temper, probably justifiably and she did think she'd killed Zona.

"Very well, what was the next move? A few minutes after six I had a telephone call. It was from Zona. He explained that he was staying in his fiat because he had a very bad cold. The voice I heard on the telephone was unlike Zona's. It sounded too harsh, but at the time I put this down to the cold that had kept him at home. I know now that it wasn't Zona telephoning--it was the murderer. He had already begun to work up the case against Meralda by pretending to be Zona, by telling me, as he did, that he had had a threatening telephone call from her that afternoon and that she'd said she would kill him. Have you got that?"

Ricket nodded.

"Well," said Gaunt, "you remember what the

hall-porter at the Colindale Apartments said. He said that at six fifty-five Zona telephoned down to him and told him to get some spirits bf alcohol. He said that he was certain it was Zona--he recognised Zona's voice. That was the real Zona, who had no cold and who was speaking in his normal voice."

Ricket whistled. He began to look very interested.

"The next question which came to my mind," the private detective went on, "is why Zona at six fifty-five should suddenly need some spirits of alcohol. Well, I know the answer to that one.

"A minute or two before, Meralda, standing on the right hand side of the desk, had pointed her automatic at him and pulled the trigger. The wad from the blank cartridge had struck Zona on the left hand side bf the head and knocked him silly for a moment. He slumped forward on the desk.

"Meralda, thinking that she had killed him, seeing the red mark on the left-hand side of his head, turned and hurried out of the flat. But in a minute or two Zona had recovered himself, and he telephoned down to the hall-porter for the spirits of alcohol to bathe the abrasion made by the wad on the left hand side of his head.

"The hall-porter says that as he had reached the doorway on his way to the chemist's to get the spirits of alcohol, the telephone rang again. It was Zona cancelling his previous instructions, saying that he didn't want it. Isn't that what the hall porter told you, Ricket?"

Ricket nodded. "That's right," he said.

"Didn't it strike you as being very strange," said Gaunt, "that Zona, who a moment or two before had decided that he wanted spirits of alcohol, now suddenly decides that he doesn't want them?"

"It did strike me that way," said Ricket. "But I could see no possible explanation."

Gaunt grinned. "I can," he said, "just after Zona had telephoned down to the hall-porter the first time, somebody entered the study from the bedroom. That person had come up by the fire-escape. It was the murderer. Zona wasn't particularly surprised and the reason was that the murderer had telephoned that afternoon to say he was coming to see him. Zona didn't want to be interrupted in the conversation he was about to have so he immediately telephoned down to the hall-porter and told him that he didn't want the spirits of alcohol."

Ricket said: "It is quite a possible theory, but why are you so certain that the murderer telephoned Zona and made the appointment?"

"That's simple," said Gaunt. "Zona had arranged that the girl Geraldine should go round to see him that afternoon. On Lanel's instructions she didn't go. She hung about and waited, the idea being that she should go round there with Lanel. At half-past six Zona telephoned through to the Silver Ring Club with a message that Geraldine was to hurry. Why did he do that? He did it because he wanted her round there and out of the way again before he kept his appointment with the murderer."

"I see," said Ricket. "Then possibly Lanel had a reason for not letting Geraldine get round there on time."

Gaunt nodded. "A very good reason," he said.

"The last point," Gaunt went on, "--that suicide set-up. Whoever it was had taken the trouble to cut through the flooring under Zona's desk and fix up that pistol with the weight tied to the string attached to the butt, had carefully rigged the whole thing up so that that pistol should be found, so that the finders--probably the police--should think that Zona might have committed suicide.

"So you see, Ricket, we're up against a very clever murderer. We're up against someone who had prepared two get-outs. One, Meralda Grey, is to be suspected of the murder and possibly convicted. Alternatively, it might be thought that Zona had committed suicide. In other words, our man is drawing two red herrings across the path of the police, making certain in the process that the real killer remains unsuspected."

Gaunt got up. "If I may," he said, "I'd like to use your telephone."

                                          Peter Cheyney

Ricket nodded. Gaunt walked over to the desk and took up the telephone. He gave Meralda Grey's number. A minute or two later she came on the line.

"Hello," said Gaunt. "Meralda, I think your worries are getting less and less every moment. Tell me, has Lanel telephoned you since I saw you last?"

"No," she said. "I've had no calls at all, except, of course, one from Michael."

Gaunt grinned. "I expect that was a nice call," he said. "What did he have to say?"

"It was rather nice," she answered. "He said that he wanted me to know that he was with me heart and soul in this terrible business and that first thing tomorrow morning he was applying for a special licence so that, come what may, we might be married at once."

Gaunt chuckled. "Marvellous," he said. "Showing that the course of true love runs straight if not exactly smooth. Goodnight, Meralda. I've got an idea I'll be in touch with you soon."

He hung up the receiver and turned to Ricket.

"I've got an appointment in my office, Ricket." he said, "at ten-fifteen tonight. I want you to come along at about ten-twenty. You'll find the street door open. Come up and go into the outer office. I shall be in my private office with my caller. There's a ventilator between my own room and the outer room. I suggest that you listen. You might be very interested. And," he concluded, "I think before another twelve hours are passed you'll have your man."

XIII. -- Interview with Death

IT was ten o'clock. A high wind had sprung up. It blew the rain against the windows of Gaunt's office as he sat before a typewriter, carefully typing a letter to himself. Every now and then he paused and read what he had written. Eventually he finished, sat back and read through the complete letter, folded it, put it into his breast pocket.

It was ten-fifteen exactly when he heard the footsteps in the passage outside. Gaunt listened. Then, as he heard the knock on the door that led from his office to the passage, he got up, walked across the zoom, unlocked the door and opened lt. Michael Lorimer stood outside.

"Come in, Lorimer," said Gaunt cheerfully. He went back to his desk, sat down, motioned Lorimer to the chair opposite.

"There's no need for you to bother to ask the question that's on the tip of your tongue," said Gaunt. "Meralda's safe. I know that she didn't kill Zona. In half an hour the police will know. They'll have the murderer."

Lorimer said: "Did you get that letter? The one that the hall porter at the Colindale forgot to send you. The one he was supposed to bring round here tonight"

Gaunt nodded. He put his hand into his breast pocket and brought out the letter he had just finished typing.

He said: "I'll read it to you. This it the letter that Zona wrote to me on the afternoon of his death. I imagine that he wrote it soon after six o'clock. Listen..." He began to read:

Dear Gaunt,

Although you are coming to see me at seven-thirty tonight, I'm writing this note to you to tell you what has transpired to-day. Last night I told you that I couldn't get rid of Lorimer because he might know too much. Well, he knows a great deal. A few minutes ago he telephoned me. He's just arrived in town from Manchester. He caught the two o'clock train and apparently telephoned from Euston Station immediately he arrived.

I'm not going to tell you exactly what he said on the telephone because that would take too long, but he's trying to blackmail me. He told me that unless I arranged to hand over a considerable sum of money he would fix it that I went to prison. I think that a great deal of this was bluff, but I'm scared. At first I was inclined to refuse to see him, but on second thoughts I thought it might be more clever to hear what he has to say. I imagine he's on his way round here now. He was careful to tell me that I had better not tell anyone of his proposed visit.

I didn't like his attitude on the telephone. It scared me. And I am writing this letter to you so that if anything happens you'll know who is responsible. Possibly this sounds rather dramatic, but since I saw you last I've made a discovery that rather frightens me.

Two or three days ago Lanel, my secretary, told me that when he had come round to the flat one day he couldn't get in, and that he heard a sound something like wood being sawn. On another occasion he said he found the books taken from my bookshelves and lying on the floor.

Today I took a look around the flat and I find that my automatic pistol, which was kept in a recess behind the books on one of the shelves, is gone. I find also that someone has sawn a hole under my desk, and the gun is hanging on a string down this hole over a nail. There is a paper-weight on the other end of the string. I'm leaving all this business for you to see when you get round here tonight.

I feel that Lorimer is up to no good. I'm scared. Yours,
Mario Zona

Gaunt threw the letter on to his desk. He was smiling quite pleasantly.

"That doesn't look so good for you, does it, Lorimer?" he said.

Lorimer gave an exclamation of disgust.

"It's rubbish," he said. "Some scheme of Zona's to get me into trouble with the police. I--"

Gaunt got up. "

Save your breath," he said. "You killed Zona. You know it and I know it, so why bother to argue?"

Lorimer began to grin.

He said: "Really! Perhaps you'd like to tell me how I did it. I know nothing about it. I was in Manchester. Lanel can prove that."

"Nonsense," said Gaunt. "Lanel spoke to you in Manchester at lunch time. You left after that. You left on the two o'clock train. You arrived in London at six o'clock. You telephoned Zona from the station. And you telephoned to me too. You came through to my office. You disguised your voice. You said that you were Zona and that you'd had a threatening call from Meralda Grey. That was clever.

                    Peter Cheyney

"After giving her that gun on the pretext that she might need protection, and knowing that she was going round to see Zona soon after you'd arranged to drop in on him yourself, you knew perfectly well that she'd be suspected of the murder. The joke was that that poor girl very nearly killed Zona. Luckily, I'd reloaded the gun with blank ammunition."

"I see," said Lorimer, with a sarcastic smile. "Supposing for the sake of argument that I had intended to drop in on Zona, do you think that I should be such a fool as to telephone him first?"

"You had to telephone him first,", said Gaunt coolly, taking out his cigarette case and extracting a cigarette. "You had to telephone him first so that you would know he'd be alone when you arrived. Zona had a date with one of the cigarette-girls from the club--Geraldine. After your telephone call he rang through to the club to tell her to hurry round. That was so that she should be there when you arrived. Zona thought that if there was someone else there he'd be safer, even if it was only a girl. He knew you daren't try to be tough if he wasn't alone."

Lorimer said: "Well, that more or less lets me out. If Geraldine went round to Zona's flat and didn't see me there nobody can prove that I was there. You're bluffing, Gaunt."

"Am I?" said Gaunt coolly. "I'm not bluffing, and you know it. Geraldine was late going round to

Zona's place because Lanel made her late. And he made her late because he knew you were going to be there. You told him by telephone from Manchester that you were going to see Zona when he told you about finding Zona's will; that Zona had left a lot of money to Meralda Grey. Lanel wondered what was going to happen at that interview. He knew that you were going to get what you could out of Zona, more especially as Zona would cancel that will at the first opportunity. Well, he didn't get a chance to cancel it. You killed him first, and Meralda Grey is an heiress, which is the reason why you telephoned through to her tonight and told her that you were getting a special licence to marry her tomorrow."

Gaunt paused to let the next words sink in. "So that you would get that money after she'd been hanged for killing Zona."

Lorimer looked at the detective. His eyes were narrow slits.

"You've got a certain amount of brains, I must say, Gaunt," he said. "I hope they'll be of use to you."

"I expect they will," said Gaunt with a smile. "But perhaps you'd be interested if I told you just what happened at Zona's flat at six-fifty yesterday?"

He stubbed out his cigarette. "You hung about for a bit after you'd telephoned to Zona first of all, and then to me pretending you were Zona with a bad cold. Then you went along to the Colindale Apartments. You saw Meralda go in the front entrance. You cut round to the back, ran along the passage and went up the fire-escape. You went through the double windows into the bedroom. You listened to the short and sharp quarrel between Meralda and Zona. You saw her point the pistol at him, you saw him slump over the desk, and you saw her go. You must have felt awfully pleased to think that she'd killed him for you--and you must have been awfully surprised when you saw Zona pull himself together and telephone down to the hall-porter for some spirits of alcohol."

Gaunt lit another cigarette coolly. "You thought you'd better do something about it. So you stepped into the room. You had a gun in your hand. You ordered Zona to telephone down to the hall-porter and tell him not to bother about getting the spirits of alcohol."

Lorimer grinned evilly. "You're a good guesser, Gaunt," he said. "Go on; you interest me!"

"I'm glad of that," said Gaunt . "Well, to continue: Zona was pretty scared. You told him that you wanted some money--big money--and that you intended to have it or else you were going to say what you knew about him. Zona retaliated by telling you that any illegal business in the clubs had been started by you, possibly in conjunction with

Lanel; that he had brought me in to look after him and that he wasn't paying any blackmail money."

Gaunt blew a smoke ring and watched it sail across the office. Then he went on: "You didn't mind about that a bit. You told Zona that if he didn't come across then and there you were going to kill him. You told him how you'd given a 0.32 gun to Meralda that morning for her own protection; that you had just seen her leave the flat, and that if you killed Zona she would be suspected; that you yourself had an alibi--you were in Manchester. Brickett had seen you there and Lanel had talked to you on the telephone there.

"Zona played for time. He was hoping that Geraldine would arrive and create a diversion. You realised that you'd got to get the job over quickly. After all you had to get back to Manchester again to make your alibi perfect. You shot Zona. You were just about to go when you had a brainwave. Lanel had told you on the telephone about Zona's will leaving the money to Meralda. You remembered the suicide set-up you had fixed up under the floor with Zona's own gun. If you could make it appear that Zona had committed suicide you'd have Meralda and the money he'd left her.

"You moved Zona, got down under the desk, pulled up the suicide gun on the string and put it in Zona's hand, while you were doing this Lanel

                                        Peter Cheyney

arrived. He came up the fire-escape and saw you through the open door of the study. You didn't see him. You were just putting the gun into Zona's hand. Lanel turned and started to go back down the fire-escape. On the way down he saw Geraldine coming. He went down pretending he hadn't seen her, went to the other end of the passage, and then returned after she'd been in the bedroom and seen Zona's arm and shoulder slumped over the desk with his hand holding the gun. Lanel said: 'My God, let's get out of this' because he knew you were still in the flat. He'd already made up his mind to say nothing and, if the police thought it was suicide, to split the legacy left to Meralda with you."

Lorimer said. "You know, Gaunt, you're not a bad detective!"

Gaunt grinned. He said: "You're telling me! Unfortunately for Lanel's scheme I forced his hand. I bluffed a confession out of Geraldine that she had been round to Zona's place. I pretended that there was a possible case against her.

"That frightened Lanel badly. He's keen on Geraldine. He knew this time the police would not accept the suicide theory, because, unfortunately for you, soon after you had left Zona's place rigor mortis began to set in. The body slipped off the chair where you had left it and fell by the side of the desk, and the suicide gun, dragged by the paper-weight, had fallen down the hole under the desk.

"All Lanel wanted to do was to protect Geraldine and himself. But he didn't want to give you away. He wanted to split that money with you. Therefore he was forced to play into my hands and try to throw suspicion on Meralda by going to the police and telling them that I had loaded the blank ammunition into her gun after the killing. This didn't worry me because I always knew that I could prove that I did it before the murder.

"But the fact that Lanel did this showed me that he was working in conjunction with you."

Gaunt stubbed out his cigarette, leant back in his chair and relaxed. His eyes were on Lorimer.

Lorimer said: "You've got it nearly dead right. It was unlucky that Zona wrote that note to you."

Gaunt grinned. "He didn't," he said coolly. "He never wrote me any note. I typed that letter to myself on the machine here just before you came. I knew when I told you over the telephone that Zona had written me a note and that the hall-porter hadn't delivered it, but that I should have it tonight, that you'd have to come 'round here to get it.

"You knew that if Zona had written a note after six o'clock when you telephoned him, that he would mention the fact that you were coming to see him, and that that would spoil your Manchester alibi. You came round here tonight to get that note."

                    Peter Cheyney

Lorimer put his hand into his overcoat pocket. When it came out it held an automatic. Lorimer held the gun, quite steadily, levelled at Gaunt's head.

"You're quite right, Gaunt," he said. "I did come round for that note and I'm going to have it, no matter who wrote it. You know too much for me. I've still got a chance to make a getaway, but I'm going to get you first. I killed Zona and I'm going to kill you."

Gaunt said: "That's fine."

He glanced at his wrist-watch. It was twenty-five minutes past ten. His ears, straining for every sound, heard an almost inaudible movement from the outer office.

He said quite calmly: "Well... That's too bad for me. But before you start on the killing process I'd just like you to listen to me for a minute. I'm quite prepared to make a deal with you over this business. We might still be able to hang it on Lanel."

"Really," said Lorimer, "That's interesting. And how would you manage that?"

Gaunt said: "Listen to this..." He began to talk rather loudly and rapidly as the door leading to the outer office began to open softly.

"This is how we could manage it," said Gaunt. He reached for the cigarette box, took one, and pushed the box towards Lorimer. As Lorimer reached with his free hand for a cigarette, Ricket shot through the door and jumped at Lorimer's back. At the same moment Gaunt ducked down as Lorimer pressed the trigger of the automatic. The bullet whistled over Gaunt's head.

Gaunt got to his feet as Ricket, with a vicious right swing, smashed Lorimer to the floor. He lay there unconscious.

Gaunt lit his cigarette. Ricket put his hand into his hip pocket and produced a pair of handcuffs. He slipped them over the wrists of the unconscious murderer. Then he mopped his brow.

"That was a close thing," he said. "I thought you were for it this time, Rufus."

Gaunt smiled. "So did I," he said. "Well, Ricket, you've got your murderer and you heard my own story. I hope you found it interesting."

"Very interesting," said Ricket. "And I agree with one thing he said 100 per cent. I think you're a damned good detective, too! However, we'll discuss that later. In the meantime I'm going to telephone for a police car to take this so-and-so to a nice cosy cell." He went to the telephone.

Gaunt got up. He put on his hat. "I've got a date," he said. "I'll leave you to look after Lorimer. Let me know if you need me, Ricket, and shut the office door after you go, and the downstairs door."

Ricket, grinned. "All right," he said, "I'll look

after it. But you're in a devil of a hurry to get off somewhere, aren't you?"

"Why not?" said Gaunt. He was grinning. "What do you think I've taken all this trouble for? Why do you think I chanced this fellow having a shot at me?"

Ricket laughed. "You mean Meralda Grey?" he said.

"Right, Sherlock," said Gaunt. "I'm going round to see her. I'm going to tell her that she can sleep soundly tonight. And I'm going to tell her one or two other things, too, that are no business of yours."

Lorimer began to stir. From outside came the sound of the police car pulling up.

Ricket said humorously: "Well, ask me to the wedding. But I must say, Rufus, I never expected to see you falling for a woman with a temper like Meralda's."

Gaunt grinned again. He said: "I'm a glutton for punishment."

He went out, whistling softly.

THE END

A story from

Stories reflecting today
Yabot AB
www.yabot.se

Peter Cheyney

www.ingramcontent.com/pod-product-compliance
Lightning Source LLC
LaVergne TN
LVHW011014200726
843509LV00011B/1091